Praise and Reviews

★ ★ ★ ★ ★

"A fascinating look at the possibilities of the future, the bleak and the beautiful.   A tale we could use about right now."

-   Richard Bates

"I really hated Maria, she is a world-class villain. I really understand why no one would want to claim her as a grandma."

-   Anita Gutierrez

"Is everyone in this book gay?"

-   A. Vargas Nieto

"A true genre-bender! This dystopian sci-fi novel set in Kansas introduces readers to a mesmerizing world of augmented reality, where three women's destinies intertwine in unexpected ways."

-   ChatGPT (probably)

-

"Vonnegut meets Orwell! A fantastic story with interesting characters and a good twist. Highly recommended 5 stars. I cannot wait for the next MJ Douglas book."

- Instagram Review

"If you're in the mood for a wild ride into a future of augmented reality, filled with moments that will make you burst into laughter, this book is a must-read."

- Reedsy Review

"My favorite character was Rhonda. She brought a depth to the world that worked for me. Five stars."

- Fluff (probably)

"This book takes you on a wild ride that is absolutely a potential future for humanity. Technology is amazing, but at what cost? We need to be asking ourselves these questions now at the advent of generative AI."

- Maria Gutierrez

"A thrilling rollercoaster of emotions! This novel seamlessly blends technology and human emotions, making it a must-read for anyone intrigued by the possibilities of augmented reality."

- Robin Hall AI persona

"An entertaining cyberpunkish dystopian story."

- GoodReads Review

Augmented
By MJ Douglas

Dragon Tomes Publishing

Additional Titles by

MJ Douglas

Water Rites (short story)

Echo (late 2023)

Thank you for buying this Dragon Tomes
Publishing book.

To receive special offers, bonus content, and info on
new releases and other great reads, sign up for our
newsletters.

Visit us online at
www.dragontomespublishing.com

Dragon Tomes Publishing
www.dragontomespublishing.com

Names: Douglas, MJ, author
Title: Augmented / MJ Douglas
Description: First edition / Kansas: Dragon Tomes Publishing, 2023
ISBN: 9781963198003
Subject: Science Fiction / Dystopian Fiction
Cover Design: El Mourtaji Noureddine
Author Illustration: Shane Delaney

Augmented

Dedication

To my parents who always believed I would and
Jen Kirmer, my spouse, who insisted I should and
graciously helped make the time for it.

Thank you.

Augmented

"You have nothing to worry about. A limitless tomorrow awaits."

– Generative AI
when asked about the future of humanity

Augmented

Prologue

Olivia

"Any last words?"

Maria's hand hovered over the execute button. It'd always been risky to send bursts of information to their network of hackers. The news recently had turned for the worse. Raids, arrests, executions. The government had been cracking down on anyone not toeing the line of legality.

Olivia smiled at her wife. The kid was asleep, and the two of them had continued to dare their dream of hitting reset on the world. It'd been Olivia's dream, her mission, her Cause. She'd never hoped to share it with someone, and here Maria was.

"Go ahead. I'll get us some tea. Perhaps we have not reached the end of our night?"

Maria's face glowed with a dashing smile. Dimples peeked out from her otherwise hawkish face. Olivia headed to the small kitchen, rummaging through the cabinet for a tin of potent tea, one of her prized possessions.

"Hitting in three. One. Two. Three."

Usually, the power dimmed as the burst swept through their equipment. Olivia waited for the spike of anxiety to pass.

Their lighting dimmed momentarily and flared

with an intensity that quickly had bulbs popping.

Olivia gave a quick scream as the light bulb in the kitchen blew, sprinkling her with glass and filament. Rose started crying from her bedroom.

Olivia's parenting instincts set in before she even knew what was happening. She ran to Rose's bedroom, quickly glancing at Maria, who was frantically hitting buttons on her keyboard.

"Hey, little bird, it's okay," she brought the child to her chest. The nine-year-olds birthday was coming soon, but she wasn't yet out of the kid stage.

Maria swore from the other room.

Olivia made soothing sounds as panic rose in her chest.

"You have to go," Maria was suddenly at the door with their coats, "You have to go, now."

Olivia stood, reacting to the order by putting the coat on Rose. She wanted to ask why, but Maria had already started removing the air vent cover. Olivia had insisted on a residence that had a secondary exit. In their line of work, one couldn't be too careful.

"What about Terminus?" she couldn't help to ask as she pushed Rose into the vent.

"It's gone. They starburst us," the light exploding made sense. As did the acrid smell of burnt electronics.

Olivia's heart sank. Her life's work was gone. She handed Rose a flashlight.

"Go on. You know the drill. We'll be right behind you." The girl's face drew resolute as she turned down the small corridor.

Maria pushed her towards the vent, "You'll be right behind her. I've got to stay. They've got to find someone."

Olivia shook her head adamantly, "If someone has to stay, it should be me."

"I love you. You know they wouldn't believe you were a singular actor. Go."

Noise could be heard from their front door. Olivia was out of time, and Rose needed someone. She turned and began her journey down the vent that exited into the complex's basement. It wasn't guaranteed that they wouldn't be caught, either. Maria replaced the vent cover.

She could vaguely hear, moments later, the front door breaking and Maria's raised voice demanding an explanation.

Olivia and Rose had spent the evening in the basement of the apartment complex doing a bag of laundry they'd hidden for just such a reason. The military police had popped down briefly, flashlight evaluating them as non-threatening, and left.

Olivia was shaken. She didn't dare return to their apartment. It was probably under surveillance.

"Come on, love. We're going to get a hotel for the night."

"What about Mama?"

Olivia didn't respond. Maria was dead to them both.

The next morning was rough. Crying for a bit of the night hadn't done her much good outside of waking up with a headache and crusty eyes. She ordered room service and tried to decide what to do.

They'd been planning Terminus together for

years. The program that would save humanity. Olivia had not thought it was possible until she met Maria.

The woman was a once-in-a-century genius regarding Network infiltration and artificial intelligence. Olivia realized what she had on her hands when she'd tried to pin her down to recruit her for the Cause ten years prior.

At that point, they were just a tiny hacktivist group with vision, politics, and a little skill. It'd taken the entire team to track Maria down, and the only reason the woman had let them approach was because she was interested in Olivia.

They were a match made to change the world. Except Maria was in prison, likely on the list for treason. Olivia petted Rose's hair as she thought about the future.

She'd known for a long time that though Terminus was her dream, Maria was the only one capable of executing it. She brought up her backup augmented reality office space and tapped some commands on the workspace keyboard.

"You called?" they'd created a revolutionary AI personality a few years back.

"Hey, love. We've been compromised. Are you clean?"

Time passed. The food was delivered to the room, and Rose happily munched artificial pancakes. Olivia watched as her kid ate the nutrient paste printed to look like old-fashioned pancakes.

"Confirmed. They starburst Maria's lab to find her. They had not infiltrated our systems. I am on the beta-three backup terminal."

Small miracles.

"Do you have data on Maria?"

"Affirmative. She's being held in District 3, in a retention cell on death row for those who have committed treason."

Even expected, it still made Olivia's heart clench.

"We've got to change her sentencing."

The AI paused in its response. Olivia knew there were a few variables to process. She brought up the virtual representation of the prison tracking system on her interface.

"The likelihood of this succeeding without you being caught is minimal."

Olivia knew. This wasn't a save-the-day scenario. This was a hard swap. She'd trade her life for Maria's. She hugged Rose for a moment. She regretted her insistence on having a kid. Life was not going to be easy for the child.

"I know. We need Maria free."

They worked for the next three weeks on the plan. The execution. The attempt to hide from authorities. None of the planning mattered. Once they'd infiltrated the prison system, a tracer had been attached to their location. The AI could melt into the Network and disappear to their delta site. Olivia was all too real, all too human.

They'd hauled her off with one last message bleeding into her earpiece. It was in the AI's voice, just a whisper.

"It worked."

Olivia's dreams of revolution had steeled her to the possibility of execution. Of not being able to see the reality she'd been working her whole life to create. She could die with the knowledge that it was still possible. That Maria was still in the world. That Rose wasn't alone.

Her heart beat loudly in her chest as the man strapped her into the chair. Her eyes looked forward, unwilling to acknowledge the circumstance. She kept her mouth shut, refusing to respond when the question was asked.

"Any last words?"

Part 1
Chris

Chapter One

Flicker

The power flickered. Chris was sitting, watching TV with her cat, Rhonda. Something they did every day. Except Rhonda was suddenly on the other side of the living room. Fur raised, a Mohawk of concern running down the animal's back.

"It's okay, Rhonda, it's just a storm," just another acid rain storm. She imagined the acidic water slowly eating through the power lines. Her imagination was ridiculous. They'd long ago buried or treated the power lines to protect against such erosion. The actual threat was falling trees, and tall trees weren't as common.

She reached for the cat, trying to calm the beast, "Come here, you scaredy cat, we're okay."

A crack of thunder hit, and the power flickered again. The cream-colored walls of her house disappeared for an instant into darkness. Chris jerked with a shiver down her spine. Maybe Rhonda had a right to be frightened. This storm was worse than usual.

"House, please switch to our generator until the storm passes."

"Acknowledged," came the robotic response. A reassuring hum came from the generators below the floorboards. They wouldn't have any more power flickers tonight. Rhonda calmed down immediately. The cat was too smart for her own good. Chris reached down and picked up the animal, rubbing the fur down to eliminate the last vestiges of fear.

Chris was still shaken up. Her spine still tingled with a sense of danger. Should she call her son? Her daughter? Was everyone okay?

"And now that you've got chicken cubes, you roll it in imitation egg, get a nice thick coating before you drop your cubes into the dehydrated crumbs," the TV crooned to her. Everyone was okay. She was as skittish as Rhonda.

Chris sat back in the recliner, which automatically formed around her body. Everything was good. She'd see Jessica tomorrow. The kid had some plans for her. The house was comforting and solid. The power flicker had been an anomaly. Everything was good. The repetition of thought was soothing.

The panic began to recede. A power outage was a serious thing. Each municipality and house had backup generators and could technically run independently. She hadn't experienced a power outage since she was a kid before the backup generators existed.

She was safe. Rhonda began to purr on her lap. The cooking show was walking through frying the chicken cubes into a tasty-looking entree. Everything was good.

Chris reached over to the table to grab the book she'd been reading. As a great fan of Gothic horror, she read books on paper instead of the digital formats most others loved. This may have made her a dinosaur, but she didn't care. The latest find was an old copy of Frankenstein, fitting for a dark, rainy night. She liked having cooking shows in the background. One can't get too frightened listening to chicken cubes fry.

Chapter Two

Acrylic Commentary

"I am a fifty-two-year-old lesbian who hasn't dated in twenty years. I'm not about to start now," Chris knew she sounded whiny, which didn't help. She didn't appreciate whining in other people, and she certainly disapproved of it coming out of her own mouth. Pathetic. It was a word she'd used to describe herself lately. Her gray hair had gotten long, shaggy. It was usually a fashionable short spiky cut. She'd been feeling old recently, and spiky didn't fit old.

"I know, Mom, but it's been two years," Chris could tell her daughter, Jessica, was trying, "Ben and I are fine. You need to live your life."

Chris shook her head. Jessica was the domineering one of her two children. Jessica had a plan almost as soon as Mia popped her out. The kid had drive, a mission. One of her most annoying quirks was the unwavering assumption that everyone else had to be just as self-possessed and motivated. She was tall and had been taller than Chris since middle school. Dark hair with warm brown eyes, just like Mia. None of these factors helped Chris stand up to her demanding child.

"I am living my life, I'm quite," she couldn't

bring herself to say happy, "content. What about you? I haven't heard you talk about anyone special in a long time. You're young, and you should put yourself out there."

"Content isn't enough, Mom. You deserve to be happy. And don't change the subject. This conversation is about you. I'm perfectly fine. You know I don't plan on settling down anytime soon. Also, I date, which is more than we can say about you," she clicked her nails against the stone countertop. They tapped, waiting for an answer, demanding an answer. Click, click, click— pink acrylic vehicles of resolve.

The kid was not going to stop. A compromise would have to be made. Chris's mind jumped from thought to thought, trying to find something to appease Jessica. Her point was valid. Jessica did date. She dated a lot. Men, women, enby, queer. Her tastes were omnivorous and sat firmly on the 'just having fun' side of the relationship scale. Sometimes Chris wished she was wired that way.

"What are you suggesting?" she spoke the words carefully in a tone that wasn't too open. She knew the statement meant she'd have to agree to something. That something was still debatable.

A well-planned pause, "You could go to a bar. A couple on the East side caters to a more mature crowd." Chris scoffed. Her, at a bar? She hadn't gone to bars when she was young, much less sitting at fifty-two. She wasn't going to find the type of relationship she wanted at a bar. Her nose wrinkled in distaste, a tell Jessica picked up on immediately.

"You could try something different, t/(s)he/y?"

Jessica knew this was an unlikely suggestion. Not that t/(s)he/y couldn't work, just that her mother was stubborn. Plus, a few friends had terrible experiences with online dating and had been very vocal about it. Jessica had stupidly gossiped with her Mother about it, poisoning the well. Granted, they were trying to date men, not lesbians, but still.

"I realize I'm hopeless, Jess. Let's admit it and move on."

"Mom, you don't have to date anyone, just meet people. A service like t/(s)he/y could let you define what you want. If you want something that's no fun, say so. If you want someone boring, write it down. Just friends? They've got that too. Get out there, and become part of the community. You'll become that Halloween costume you wore when I was eight."

Chris thought back, Halloween costume… which costume was that? Oh yes, the crazy cat lady. With a bathrobe, grey hair, a ball of yarn, and several stuffed animal cats. Jess had thought it was hilarious when she borrowed the stuffed animals. Ben, her five-year-old son, had thought she was embarrassingly crazy.

"That was low, Jess, a crazy cat lady? You know it's just me and Rhonda. You can't be a crazy cat lady with only one cat," Rhonda jumped on the counter at the sound of her name. She let an affectionate rowl and rubbed up against Chris's arm.

"But you can be a shut-in. You're practically agoraphobic."

"I'm not afraid of going out. I'm just busy with

work, with stuff," her excuses sounded flimsy, even to her. She knew she'd let things pass her by. She was able to work from home most of the time. Groceries and essentials could be delivered and most often were. Going outside didn't have much appeal. The neighborhood was run down, with weeds growing through the cracks. Driving wasn't fun anymore. The laws passed to outlaw human drivers sucked the fun from it. Kids didn't play outside. She couldn't bring herself to go to the park. It held few attractions outside of some sickly trees and a mutant, burrowing squirrel. Even the zoo was depressing, with a few 'last examples of' wildlife that had been common a hundred years ago.

"Okay," Jess elongated the vowel, exasperated, "how about that new game? You like games and technology. Get yourself a VR chip, an updated AR chip, or anything! I know you can afford to give it a try."

The idea was intriguing but didn't seem like it'd force her to meet people. She worked part-time and on call as a mainframe tech at the Network of Midwest Universities. It wasn't a glorious job. Mainframes had gone out of style eighty years ago as companies had moved to the cloud, the nebula, and finally, the Network. Many organizations had never adopted modern technology, not wanting to invest in making their application's cloud or nebula compatible. Old applications had their purpose. Even as her job was old school, so had she tended to be, preferring to read about new tech in *The Futurist* than to try it out herself.

"What new game?" still, a game was a better

suggestion than t/(s)he/y.

"There's a *Mysterio Isle*. It's a mystery set on," Jess switched tactics, sensing her Mom's disinterest, "but they also have a new scientific one. You know, where you help identify and categorize the physical world for analysis to build better algorithms for identification."

Chris was intrigued. A game that helped science sounded promising.

"I've even heard that many of these games have specific communities, so you can interact with gamers that are more in line with your interests," Jess was trying to sound bland. She'd realized the relationship angle wasn't as appealing to Chris as science.

Chris teetered on the fence. It did spark her interest.

"I'll even help get it all set up," Jess offered. This tipped Chris into acceptance. Setting up technology was one of the things she'd relied on Mia for years. It was a personal pet peeve that technology required so much effort to get going. Plus, this was a full-circle moment. She remembered getting her parents on their first Wii and the time it took to sync their remotes every couple of months— one of the few perks of having kids.

"Alright, alright, let's go out tomorrow night. We can buy one of these new chips tomorrow. A new AR chip, though, the full VR experience creeps me out."

Jessica tried to hide her glee and only partially succeeded, "Sounds good, I'll pick you up at 6, and we can do dinner."

"End call," Chris disconnected her holographic phone, shaking her head. The virtual image of Jess pixelated and dissolved. She'd adopted many new technologies, voice-operated systems for her house, a self-driving car, and enthusiastically embraced a self-cleaning litter box. She even used, limitedly, an augmented reality chip. It was old school, one had to wear special contacts, and it was only helpful outside her house. She had never been interested in Virtual Reality. To some, it was like a drug. People got so caught up in their VR universe that they lost all concept of their real lives. She didn't want to escape from her life. She just needed distraction from the monotony of it. Maybe even to find excitement in it again. A game could be fun. She'd been into AR games when they were first introduced, but Mia and the kids had stolen the time required for those activities. A game that helped scientific advancement played on her sensibilities.

Augmented reality had advantages since it operated in the real world. It was an upgraded version of the world where people could put virtual statements on the Network for all to see. The games and scientific tools interacted with what the user saw, creating additions to reality. The story pursued would be a work of fiction, but the computer was intelligent enough to make the mystery within the existing world. Searching a dungeon for the three hidden keys became searching the neighborhood for the three hidden keys. It had the potential to make life new again. One could go for a walk with a pet dragon and bump into a neighbor with their unicorn.

Chris read that it had the potential to make the mundane enjoyable if a person could get over the inherent silliness of walking a dragon. Which, until now, she'd considered beyond her imaginative capabilities.

If nothing else, she'd humor Jess. It couldn't hurt. It had been a while since she'd been out of the house for anything but work or the occasional grocery run. She'd never want agoraphobia to be a term applied to her. With a puff of air, she blew her long bangs out of her eyes- maybe it was time for a haircut too.

Chapter Three

Disconnected

Chris's day came and went with an undercurrent of anxiety. Her mouth was sour and dry. No matter how much water she drank, she couldn't eliminate the taste of fear. She logged into work, watching the systems run. She was waspish with her fellow employees on the Link. She grumped at Rhonda, who kept lying on the keyboard as she typed in commands. She made several errors in her querying and had to restart her capacity analysis twice. It wasn't a good day.

Given her profession, it was ironic that she'd resisted technology most of her life. She had a good job, a rarity in the modern world. Tech jobs were the only ones that paid. Not that it mattered. Even for those who didn't work, the standard of living wasn't bad. Not compared to the early days of the digital revolution. Her technology ambivalence, or outright stubbornness, had always been a bone of contention with her ex-wife. This was why she didn't give her kids much credit in the argument. Mia was always messing with her life indirectly. For having walked out on her, the woman was downright obsessed.

She'd done some research online. AR has

become more sophisticated in the last five years. Scientific augmentation was a real thing. An application called The Zoo could be downloaded. The app was used to classify objects in the real world for input into a massive database. It was identifying plants, taking snapshots of objects, and flicking left or right depending on potential categories. Things it would take a million researchers years to accomplish could be done by an army of decisive gamers. Real advancements in understanding the state of the world's ecology could be made. Scientists could identify actions and policies based on the data that could theoretically change the ecology. With this technology, the app boasted they could save the world! If the world weren't dead already, that might have been possible.

Before competing with the heavy gamer crowd, the app had a way to go. It rewarded players with trophies, titles, and sometimes money. It was a hit from the reviews, although she had difficulty trusting a 4.9-star rating. Reviews could be faked. But working on a cosmic question while plugged in was romantic. One could even explore the galaxy, floating around the heavens and classifying astronomical phenomena. Flick to the left for a red star, the right for a comet, and up for a galaxy. Satellites have spun around the Earth for over a century, taking millions of pictures that have yet to be analyzed. Astronomers had photos that would take thousands of years to analyze. Not anymore, not with a crowd.

Chris unplugged for the day. It'd been

uneventful. Batch jobs ran unobtrusively. Everything connected perfectly, and there were no reported intrusions to investigate. Rhonda purred on her lap. She sat stroking the silky fur, listening to the low rumble. She leaned back in the chair, stretching her cramped legs, closing her eyes. The antique clock ticked with its competitive nature challenging the solitude, the timelessness of being alone.

When Mia first moved out, Chris couldn't stand being alone. She'd always had the TV going or the online radio. She'd constantly talk to Rhonda and have the kids out every weekend. It wasn't so much the aloneness as much the quiet. Too much quiet, her mind would chase itself into the corners of the rooms choking on the dust bunnies. Except there weren't any dust bunnies. The house was immaculate, the shutters replaced, the windows clean. The toilet had even been scrubbed with a toothbrush. She didn't know when the noise receded, but eventually, she learned how to be alone. She learned it too well, according to Jessica.

"You ready?" came the intercom-ed voice of her daughter in the impatient cadence of youth.

"Coming," Chris replied, giving a few last commands to her house, "House, feed Rhonda. Lights out. Alarm on in two minutes."

"Rhonda. Lights. Alarm. Acknowledged," came the smooth robotic voice Chris associated with her household affairs. She heard the electronic deadbolt slide into place three steps away from the house. Four more steps took her past the hedge bushes and into view of her daughter's car. The Model Z sat quietly, waiting for her presence. The smog-inducing cars of her youth had been surpassed by these streamlined, battery-run, silent vehicles. She took a deep breath as she got in. She'd never been entirely comfortable in an automated car. She'd resisted until last year they started threatening jail time for anyone caught physically driving their car. The only exceptions to the law were "classic car" weekends. They insisted that not only was driving yourself unsafe, but it also messed with the algorithms and safety of self-driving cars. Some day, in the not-so-distant future, human-driving cars will be relegated to museums and junkyards- a relic of a long-forgotten past.

"Good evening, Jess."

"Hi, Mom. Ready to go?"

"Sure," she replied as the automatic seatbelt slipped into place. Did she have a choice? This distinctly seemed like something Jessica was going to push and push until it happened. Some things were easier to go along with and throw in a drawer than outright resist.

"Barb, take us to TechNow."

The car acknowledged receipt of the command and slipped into gear. Chris never got used to NextGen's ability to name their devices. Jessica had a car named Barb, a plugged-in apartment called Juan, and a personal assistant chip, Latoya. Chris had her house and car voice-activated. She'd turned off the assistant in her chip and had manually manipulated her environment with hand commands. She pretended to flick at the old cell interface she no longer owned. Chris had been weirded out when the AI "assistant" asked if she wanted to add toilet paper to the grocery list. She didn't want anyone tracking her TP usage. No one needed to know when she was out of TP but her.

The car merged into traffic seamlessly. When the laws changed several years ago, Chris reluctantly bought a self-driving car. Insurance companies weren't obligated to offer insurance on personal drivers, creating an immediate astronomical increase in the cost of private insurance. Even so, her car had personality. She'd grown used to its quirks. It was disconcerting to be in Jess's new, upgraded car. It moved with inhuman grace. Not feline, not earthly, but like a puddle of mercury rolling across a hand. Dangerous, beautiful like an Alien's reptilian grace before it burst out an extra head covered in metallic teeth. Jessica accepted it without question, as did most members of the NextGen. Chris clutched the "oh Jesus" bar on the car door, knuckles whitening as the vehicle hit 120 mph. She briefly wondered if Jesus had any thoughts about automated death machines.

"We'll be there soon," Jessica told her, as though that would comfort her. They would be there soon because the car was speeding at 150 mph in robust traffic. They would be there soon because everywhere was close at those speeds.

Trees flew by too quickly to identify. One car passed them with only a dog as a passenger. It looked like those turn-of-the-century images where they edited photographs to make it look like the dog was driving. Except now they could: Ralph could request his four o'clock drive. She almost asked,

"Did you see that?" but it was evident that Jess hadn't. She was too busy applying makeup. Why would Jess pay attention when she didn't have to?

Too soon, they arrived. The car pulled into a parking spot with perfect precision. Parallel parking had always been a struggle for Chris. Heck, parking generally was a challenge. Mia complained that her parking was always crooked, on the line, or not pulled in far enough. The litany of complaints caused a self-fulfilling prophecy of anxious parking. Two years later, she was still sabotaged by the thought of Mia. She shook her head. This trip to TechNow was about the future, not the past.

Jessica strode into the technology store as though she owned the place. It was a stand-alone store that, a hundred years ago, would have taken up the space of a giant warehouse. Now it was slightly bigger than a taco shack.

The NextGen crowd connected to technology in ways undreamed by other generations. In a way, she did own the store. It was her domain. The Next Generation owned technology at a level of personalization only imagined in a sci-fi utopia or dystopia, depending on how it was examined.

"I'm interested in a P46 chipset," Jess wasn't one for pleasantries. She went straight to the point.

"You have a P46. What is the purpose of your second set, a backup?"

Jess shook her head, "No, it's for my Mom," she pulled Chris forward. The salesperson looked at her critically. She was used to the pitying look. Her older masculine features and hair weren't in style for a woman, a mom, or even, these days, a lesbian.

"I see," the man gave Jess a look of sympathy that made Chris want to pop him in the nose. He gave his chip a couple of hand commands setting some scanners running, "Ma'am, please turn on your current chip-set so I can analyze your settings."

She looked at him squarely, "I wear a P20, and the network function is turned off." She only turned on the network functions for work. She didn't want anyone she didn't know connected to her network.

He blinked, unable to process why someone might have their network function turned off.

"She's GenZ, and I'm trying to drag her into the NextGen."

This got a knowing smile and more pity, "And what functionality do you want to get out of the P46? There isn't much you can do with it un-Networked that you can't do with a P20."

Chris bristled. She was paranoid about being continuously networked, "I'm not sure."

Jess asked the salesman, "You don't offer a limited Network model? I heard that they made a P46Sec for sensitive persons." Chris could almost hear her mouth the words 'paranoid loonies.'

Chris didn't know how she felt about being called a "sensitive person," but a more secure, limited Network version would be most welcome. If it took having this guy think she was a paranoid loony, then so be it. She had no intention of selling herself out to some AI assistant, no matter how useful they theoretically claimed to be.

"No, we don't have that in stock. We're not in LA. Plus, you add a 30% markup for the security.

But I can order a version. You can have it dropped off tomorrow by drone, bring it in, and we can help customize it."

Jess's face fell. They would not be leaving with a P46 in hand, and she knew that her chance to get Chris caught up on technology and out of her house was slipping away. It wasn't enough to have it tomorrow. She wanted it today.

"What about TechShack? Nested Solutions? Anyone in town likely to have a P46Sec?"

The sales guy gave her a sympathetic look, "I doubt it, and I'm not saying it to get a sale. Unless you're an exec, celebrity, or high profile politician," or paranoid loony, "most folks just go with the regular P46, or the A46 with all the ads."

Jess had a brief moment of disgust for her Mom and the narrow-mindedness that boxed her in. It flashed across her face in a moment and was quickly squashed. She owed this woman so much.

Chris saw and recognized both the frustration and love. Jess was NextGen but had been raised right. The kid was obsessed with technology but cared for her family deeply.

"You might try Compute Inc."

Their eyes knitted together, trying to place Compute Inc. in the town's landscape.

"Are you talking about that computer store over on 54th? The one in the old retro strip mall, with the vape vendor?"

"Yes, I know, it's a long shot. But they work with old technology and are used to folks who are a bit more… suspicious," he paused, "or, ahem, cautious," he'd edited out a few other words from his commentary.

Jessica gave a curt nod, and they turned to leave.

"You think this is worth all the effort?"

"Mom, you are worth the effort."

The statement settled it. Although Chris didn't necessarily like her worth being associated with a piece of technology, it *was* the future. A person's worth was measured in their innate ability to master the technology and to own the latest version as much as anything else. It would make her daughter feel better. Chris would give it a try, a wholehearted effort, and if it didn't work out… there was always the junk drawer.

The car didn't have Compute Inc. in its database of standard locations. They had to wait a moment as it linked to the Network to grab a GPS coordinate. Soon, they were whipping through the city, zipping down streets and turning on a dime. At some point in history, Bath was a suburb of East Saint Louis, a commuter town with tree-lined boulevards. Now the city was a quagmire of urban development. Strip malls had been converted into three-story apartments and service-based shopping complexes. With square footage plus the sidewalk, most trees abutting the street had been demolished. City trees were out of style anyway. They tended to be spindly, sickly things wedged between concrete and sewers. Instead, slow-growing bushes were the rage, and the bushes in this part of town were wild things, growing in obscene directions. They were filled with trash and reached out to passersby with gnarled limbs. They were the modern gargoyles guarding buildings with grotesque obstinance.

The car parked perfectly on a marked spot between two SUVs abutting an overgrown bush. Chris eyed the plant, idly wondering if it would eat her when she opened the door. Its crevasses held rotting paper and fast food cups. As she cracked the door, it reeked of piss.

"Are we sure this is the right place?" she asked, hoping for a negative answer.

"Oh, come on, just hop out on my side. We're in the right place, look," she pointed at a pink neon sign that Chris assumed spelled Compute Inc., although she couldn't be sure between the bush and the burnt-out letters.

A few cuss words later, Chris finished wriggling her way past the bush in front of the car. With no steering wheel or gas pedal, it was possible to exit on Jess's side of the car, but years of driving real vehicles didn't allow it to be a viable option. Taking inventory, she decided she'd gotten through with minimal damage to her coat and smelled fine. Unconsciously she brushed at her clothes as though friction could remove germs.

"Let's go," Jessica insisted, showing more enthusiasm than the dingy street warranted. The bushes took up a quarter block, a hedge of three overgrown bush monsters. The lofts were malignant growths on an old strip mall. The heavily windowed storefront was not flattering. Compute Inc. looked like an electronic dump. Peering into the windowfront, she saw old CR computer monitors piled next to LCDs. Giant desktop towers sat blinking intermittently. The effect was that of a

1980s sci-fi movie space shuttle cockpit full of blinking lights, buttons, and screens. Overall the store was dark, contradicting the blinking "OPEN" sign. Taking a breath, she pushed open the door. It surprisingly swung inwards with little resistance causing havoc by jangling obnoxiously and throwing her off balance.

"Hello, anyone here?" Jess's voice ran out as Chris tried to right herself. It took a moment for her eyes to adjust to the dimness. The room overflowed with crap, busy flickering crap. The smell of dust and electronics was overwhelming. She could feel her sinuses start to tighten in an allergic response. Old sci-fi movie heroines hung from posters on the walls, silent sentinels of the disastrous floor room. One poster made her smile. It had a gruesome Alien creature threatening a woman holding a large automatic gun in one hand and a small child in the other. It was a favorite, a classic. Whoever owned this place was bound to be interesting.

"Back here," came an annoyed woman's voice from the back of the shop, followed by some equipment hitting the floor and a muffled curse. The woman had a mild accent. Chris paused momentarily, trying to place it.

Jess, frustrated with her hesitancy, pushed past her. They walked, navigating the maze of piles of electronic junk and folding tables. Some of it was modern. A bin of dusty-looking P20s was right next to a small tub of ancient ethernet cards. Chris realized that Jessica probably didn't know what half the items in the shop were. Old USB & C cables, HDMI, M.4 strands, and other adapters were piled next to wired routers and modems. All outdated in the new age Network. The sheer amount of metal in these was likely worth a small fortune if any thief recognized it. The wire had gone out of style forty years ago when metals became beyond precious. A tub was full of ancient petabytes of storage and several refurbished boat anchors that theoretically doubled as laptops. Most of all, old PC towers stacked like Jenga blocks dominated the landscape. Wires running to and from randomly plugged in, connected, or tangled. As far as Chris could tell, none of it had any purpose.

"Ah, you've found me," the woman in front of them stuck out a rough hand covered in cuts and minor burns. Chris could smell a sodering iron burning. The woman's hand was notably rough with calluses and wrinkles from what she assumed were burns. Chris succeeded in not looking down to examine them closer. Chris was proud of her daughter when Jessica didn't hesitate to shake the woman's hand. Jessica was a bit of a priss and germaphobe, and it was an act of will to be friendly.

"What is it you've come to my humble shop for?" The woman was to the point, with no extraneous sales pitches.

Chris examined her as Jess explained their quest for a P46Sec. She was of average height, with average-colored brown hair and average brown eyes. Her skin was dark, and she was likely biracial, possibly Hispanic. Her hands, now folded in front, were covered in white scars. The woman was young, maybe late twenties. Chris was a horrible judge of age.

"I don't have a P46Sec," the woman said bluntly, but before Jessica's face fell, she continued, "But I may have something better."

The woman ducked into her back room. Electronics shuffled around. Chris was sure she saw something fly, thrown against a wall. Quick questions flew into the air.

"You have a wireless port or a surgical port?"

"Wireless."

"What model is currently compatible with your port?"

"P19-P35, but I'm not Networked, so it could be less."

"When was the last time you updated your firmware?"

"Probably last time I was Networked, two years ago."

The woman stuck her head out the door and looked at her, "That's more dangerous than being Networked, you know? Someone could hijack your feed, and your security software is outdated."

"I don't use it much. My ex used to take care of the updates."

She grunted and returned to searching, "Have you ever experienced VR? Do you get VR sick?"

"Yes and no, but I'm not here for VR. I'm not interested in that sort of fantasy."

The woman snorted, "No, I imagine not. I'm asking because I've got a DX39Sec, and they tend to have heavier graphics than a P20. If you're susceptible to VR sickness, chances are this will also make you sick."

She brought the chip forward. It was coated in

blue metallic paint, giving it a high-end look. The chip was a centimeter squared and a few millimeters thick. In a world where modern chips were unobtrusive and dull, the chip glinted in fluorescent light like a piece of the future. It was a hot rod, slicked up and ready to hit the road— an old hot rod.

"I think it's too small for my current port."

"I've got an adapter, and if you like the chip, I'd suggest you come back in a couple of weeks for a port upgrade." Chris thought this was rather presumptuous. The gritty shop was the last place she wanted to upgrade her personware.

"Look, I know you're a late adopter. This chip will last years and has the security you're looking for, but you'll only get half the experience with outdated personware. Plus, it will take me two weeks to order the stuff."

"Two weeks?" Jess was surprised. Most things could be ordered and delivered in a day or two.

"Yes, I don't peddle in ware that could be corrupted through middlemen. Half the stuff you order off those public sites comes from The Pacific Republic or someone's garage. I wouldn't put a person at risk with second-rate personware. And this is older," she paused for a second on older, "it's harder to find compatible personware." Chris wondered how many garages this woman referred to were cleaner than the shop. Still, the odd woman spoke with a tone that engendered trust and confidence. She liked the sound of avoiding 'second-rate' personware.

Chris began to appreciate this strange little

woman, "Ok, how much?"

The woman looked at her shrewdly, "Well, I've refurbed this one myself. Took off the bloat, optimized the settings for speed, and ensured the Sec profiles. Plus, a DX39Sec is tough to find. $1500."

Jess was outraged for her, "$1500 for a refurb? I could get in a P46Sec tomorrow for $1300."

"That may be, but it'd be bloated and take several days to set up for your mother. This one is set up and was only lightly used by its previous owner. Plus DX39Sec is one of the most secure models on the Network."

"Who was the previous owner?" Chris blurted out. The new fear of wearing someone else's chip dominated her mind. She'd never considered *used* personware before.

The woman looked at her, brown eyes calm, "My Grandmama was as suspicious of tech as you. And yes, I've wiped it. She was paranoid about security, so I ensured her chip was clean and secure."

Chris wondered what the woman used now.

As if reading her mind, the shop tech continued, "She's dead, so she doesn't need it now," Dead? It'd be like wearing the clothes of a dead woman. Sure, that was always possible when shopping for used clothes, but no one wanted to know. She didn't want to think about it. "Look, I'm not going to budge on the price," Chris hesitated, "$1500 is my best offer, but I'll let you return it if you don't like it within two weeks. You won't get that from a mainstream store. Plus, I'll give you 10% off your personware if you keep it."

Jess wavered. Chris did not, "Deal, and my name is Chris." She could return it if there were a ghost in the code. Heck, if she didn't like the graphics or features or thought it was insecure, she could return it. No modern chip seller would give a generous return policy unless the chip were significantly nonfunctional. She could taste the victory. She'd play along for a couple of weeks and return it. Jess wouldn't be able to complain.

The woman's eyes smiled, "I'm Anita. You're going to love this model, Chris, I have no doubt. I pride myself on matching tech to person."

Anita slipped the chip and adapter into a small compostable bag. Chris waved her wristband over the payment terminal and responded to the total of $1650 with tax with an "affirmative" voice code. It was a lot of money, but she was long overdue. She and Jessica weaved out of the store and quickly found themselves back in the sterile car.

"Well, let's go home and give it a whirl. Barb, take us back to Moms'." The car zipped into traffic without hesitation, and Chris toyed with the bag, a mild excitement building in her stomach. For the first time since being a kid, she experienced that eve of holiday excitement. It was knowing that presents awaited the following day. The feeling was unexpected and unsettling.

"I'm surprised by you, Mom. You agreed pretty quickly to all of this."

Chris shrugged, embarrassed. Could she tell her daughter, who she'd fought for years, that this felt right? Could technology feel *right*? It didn't make sense, but she knew this chip was correct for her. Maybe she'd just needed the nudge. Previously the nudge had always come from Mia. Perhaps she was finally moving on. Maybe she was going to return it in two weeks. Maybe she wouldn't.

"I guess I'm just tired of fighting you."

Jess wasn't fooled, but there was nothing obvious to call out. Plus, she'd finally won. Her Mom was upgrading to something newer, even customized. She'd heard of the DX class. They were famous for world travelers going to countries that didn't have a reliable Net. DX meant disconnected. It worked nearly as well unplugged as it did plugged in. One could set it up to run only on their home Network, and it had enough built-in capacity, memory, and adaptiveness to predict what'd be needed next and have it prepared. The Sec settings ensured a higher level of security, a passive rather than active network setting configurable to owned networks. It was sophisticated and would easily meet the needs of her tech-slow mother. Overall, Jess felt satisfied. Her Mom would finally join the NextGen crowd.

Before they knew it, they were back at Chris' with Jess offering to come in and help set everything up. Chris declined. She wanted to do it herself, which shocked them both. Plus, from experience, there's nothing more boring than watching someone flick through settings on a new piece of tech. Jess was disappointed she couldn't flex her tech knowledge but was proud of her Mom for taking the initiative.

Chapter Four

The Dragon

"House, it's me."

The front door unlocked. She'd turned off the 'swing open' function on the networked door as soon as she'd bought it. Rhonda, the sneaky beast, frequently sat by the entrance, ready to run out. She reached out and turned the doorknob, the only one on the street. Contrary to her normal state, Rhonda came sauntering forward, sleepy eyes examining her owner. She immediately sat and began licking a daintily lifted paw. "Good afternoon, puss. How are you?"

Rrrowl. Rhonda eyed her, measuring the greeting. She put her leg down and trotted up, fluffy tail curled in welcome. Rhonda rubbed up against Chris's leg, a hearty purr filling the room. Chris bent down to pat the cat, Rhonda's mottled black and brown fur soft between her fingers. There wasn't much more satisfying than being welcomed home by Rhonda.

"House, feed Rhonda," to Rhonda's satisfaction, she heard the food dispenser. The cat disappeared into the kitchen, kibble waiting. Chris could have programmed the food dispenser to deliver at specific times, but she wanted Rhonda to associate food with her. It helped cement their bond initially, and it never hurt to remind the queen of the house where her food came from. She sat in the living room and took out the chip. Examining it, she couldn't help but admire the clean lines and metallic blue shine. Chris could never understand how individuals could opt for surgical chip readers. The idea of implanting a chip into her body was disgusting. She used a wrist link, a bracelet powered enough to connect the chip to the Network and the rest of her personware. She couldn't imagine having it implanted.

Theoretically, the surgery was low risk, not painful, and relatively common. She was, however, afraid to go under a knife. Her skin crawled at the idea of having a chip in her body. Chris didn't want to be a cyborg. She didn't want to offload her human processing power to a machine.

The chip slid into the adapter effortlessly. Anita's promise that it would be all set up seemed accurate. The effect was immediate; her augmentation contacts flashed to a blue boot screen. Data was superimposed over the view of the living room. She'd heard nightmares from Jessica's experiences. New chips that a reader wouldn't recognize. Stranding the user with a black, empty screen. Or other times, chips had trouble integrating correctly, refusing to connect with the Network, contacts, or household functions. Users would get stuck in an endless cycle of updates and settings to try to fix the unfixable.

As it was, she got the standard message: "Warning: Set up will take 30-60 minutes, and it is recommended to do this in a safe, private location. Do you wish to proceed?"

"Yes."

"Acknowledged."

Words ran across her virtual screen too fast. It reminded her of the mainframe native interface, all green screens, and low tech.

"Does your neighbor own a green dragon?"

The question was absurd. Or was it? A green dragon? A virtual green dragon? She'd heard of the virtual pets, her eyes flashed to Rhonda, but she preferred the real thing.

"Do you mean a real green dragon or a virtual one?"

"I would expect that's obvious."

She hadn't counted on a sense of humor. Technology had left her in the dust. She didn't even have a sense of humor.

"I have no idea. Let me check."

She got up and walked outside. A dragon size mound of virtual shit sat in the front yard. Horned black beetles walked confidently across the poo, rolling it along the slopes into their grass. She could almost smell the acrid stench of it. Looking to the right, a small roar was followed by a gust of flames out a window. A green snout was propped on a sill, smoke curling out of its nostrils.

"Yes, they have a dragon. Looks like it's even green." Who knew? The cussing on the weekends began to make more sense. As she looked at the house, it changed. The windows became stained glass, the bushes looked more fierce, and a princess tower blinked in and out from the attic.

"What car is parked across the street?"

She looked, and the bat-mobile was parked, "The bat-mobile. Is that their augmented car?"

It flicked back to the red sedan she was used to seeing, "No, I was just checking your visual acuity. Do you hear the helicopter?"

Suddenly the chops of blades smacked the air. Chris stepped back as a small helicopter appeared to land on her front lawn. She instinctively ducked as the blades approached her head, "Yes."

The helicopter quickly made air as it took off. Fragments of dirt, grass, and leaves flew past. Many pelted her, but she felt none of the virtual particles.

"Please go back into the house," the voice was robotic and dry, not nearly as smooth as Barb, Jessica's car.

Chris obliged. She was still awed by the display of graphics. She didn't think modern augmentation had come that far. Jess was right. She had been missing out. Chris hadn't been a part of the outside world in a long time.

"Please enter your passphrase for the home network and house system. Do you wish to override 'House' with my updated programming?"

Chris's hands tapped against the kitchen island, the painted-on finger receptors typing in her passphrase, "I w1ll embrac3 my n3w lif3." She'd created it after Mia left. She'd kept it in a failed attempt to push herself out into the world.

"I do not wish to override House yet. You are here on a trial basis." Chris caught herself referring to 'it' as 'you.' It was already hard not to see it as an anthropomorphic entity.

"Understood, this DX39Sec suggests passphrases be dual authenticated with home network access. For the next 13 days, DX39Sec should be the proximity authentication."

"What if I lose you? Do I have another choice?" Chris questioned the AI's suggestions, wondering if it could sense her apprehension.

"We can set your House system to voice recognition. This will require an upgrade to its firmware."

"Do it. I don't have an implant, so it's possible I could lose you."

"Affirmative, good decision. Firmware update complete. Please repeat your cat's name three times."

Chris was amused, "Rhonda, Rhonda, Rhonda." Using Rhonda's name was familiar, but it made her suspicious. How far had the AI already weaseled into her life?

"Voice pattern locked. Proceed with personal preferences?"

Personal preferences took twenty minutes. They walked through voice choices, moving the AI from robotic female to Scottish male and settling on North American English with a voice that sounded suspiciously like her favorite historical actress, Sigourney Weaver. Had the AI created this for her?

It probably wasn't healthy to question its motives too closely, "I'm going to call you Sig. I can give you a designation, right?"

"Affirmative designation logged."

After 'Preferences' came 'Augmented Appearances,' which sounded too much like boob implants to Chris. She realized this feature turned her neighbor's modest house into a miniature castle. Her only augmentation was to turn her car into a bat-mobile. She was trying to embrace the fun.

Her final task was to bind voice commands. It took a while as the AI had argued for less obvious choices for basic commands. It didn't want to misinterpret everyday speech as a command. Chris's favorite of these three dozen commands was 'Dragon Mode,' which flicked her visual and audio pieces from reality to everyone's public augmented reality. She looked forward to exploring the 'Dragon Mode' of life. There was a lot she'd never considered about self-expression in the 'Age of Augmentation.'

Overall it was exhausting. Endless choices, only half of which she knew anything about. Chris realized that the basic setup she'd done for her P20 years ago was so horribly out of date she could see why Jessica had been pushing her. Maybe she would figure out a way to meet people. Either way, it was time to watch several shows and call it a night.

"House, TV cooking channel," the Vid screen popped up.

"Before I enter rest mode, there is one last step to completing the setup. You must review and approve of the terms of use," Chris was tired, and she was suspicious that her new friend, Sig the AI, knew it.

"Terms of use, that sounds complicated."

"Not at all. I will scroll through them. It shouldn't take long for you to digest their content."

Chris quickly discovered how different their ideas of 'easy to digest' were as pages of legalese scrolled in front of her. She used her hand commands to scroll faster to get to the accept button and her cooking show. There it was, blinking blue.

"I accept. Now let me get to my cooking show."

"Very good. I can show you TV shows through the optical interface and adapt to remove commercials, get personalized programming, and several other features," stated the AI voice calmly.

"Maybe some other time, Sig. Tonight I want to go old school."

"Enjoy," the voice sounded almost disappointed. Chris leaned back in her brown leather recliner. The leather was old, smooth, and comforting. She felt less alone, as though Sig may as well be stretched out in a companion recliner beside her watching Monsieur Montu pour red wine into his sauteed mushrooms. Eerily comforting. It wasn't long before her regular snores cut through the electronic voices. Whether it was House or Sig, Chris was unconscious of the dimming of the lights and the slow muting of the TV. The house temperature was comfortable for a human whose only blanket was a long-haired Tortie curled up in her lap. The green, active light on her wristband blinked to a blue rest mode as Sig monitored her sleep for any aberrations. If the AI had curiosity, it would have wondered how many nights Chris fell asleep in the chair. Since it didn't, it simply created a file to track sleep location, duration, wakeful vitality, and health.

Chapter Five

Unlocked

To Chris, the next few days were a whirlwind with Sig around. After Mia left, life was muted. It wasn't that Mia was a rich source of energy or excitement. The end of their two-decade-long relationship had been brutal. She didn't miss their relationship, but she did miss having a companion. A roommate to share life with, talk about their day and offer a different perspective. With the kids grown and Mia gone, Rhonda was the only person she shared her day with regularly. As much as Chris adored the cat, she'd admit their conversations were one-sided.

Sig turned out to be much more of a companion than a cat. She had a greater appreciation for why Jess was still single. It was hard to be too lonely with the AI constantly asking you questions and sharing your day.

Sig did have a stubborn streak. After a few days, she insisted Chris sleep in bed, something she hadn't done in a long time. Overall, Sig didn't nitpick or leave dirty dishes out; she was significantly easier to live with than a real roommate. More like what she imagined having a butler would be like. An ever-present *person* to talk to. Less than a friend, but more than a cat. It was odd to think there was a niche between cat and friend.

Chris never wanted a maid or butler. She'd been lonely, but not unbearably so. Not enough to go out and hire pseudo-friends. Now she looked out her window at her neighbor's dragon, and suddenly she had questions for them. What was the dragon's name? Why a dragon? Why fake dragon poo? Wasn't it overwhelming to share your life with a giant dragon? Some days tiny Rhonda gave her a run on patience.

"Why does their princess tower flicker in and out?" she murmured to herself.

"Was that a real question, or are you simply talking to yourself?"

Chris smiled. The first few days, she'd snapped at Sig that she didn't need every question answered. The answer to "Are you a pretty kitty?" had been honest, if unflattering. Chris tended to adopt cats that were a tad ugly. Not that she'd ever admit that to Rhonda.

"Do you have an answer? I'd like to know if you do."

"Certainly, it blinks in and out due to an ongoing argument among the programming of the house's inhabitants. The younger child, Jayla, would like to have a princess tower. The older male, Dione, would prefer not to have a tower, certainly not a pink one."

Chris laughed, Dione was a man's man, and Jayla was a clever little girl, "Kudos to Jayla."

"Indeed."

"I should go ask them about the dragon. I'm curious what its name is. It has a decidedly disagreeable personality for them to put up with."

"I wouldn't if I were you," the warning was given in a matter-of-fact tone.

"Why not?"

"Because that content isn't public."

The statement baffled her. If she could see it, wasn't the content public? Wasn't private content hidden? She didn't want anyone else to see her driving around in the bat-mobile. The thought made her shiver at the violation of privacy.

"How can I see it if it's private?" If a computer program could have blinked in confusion, Sig would have.

"The TCY port that interacts with the Network for augmentation and other parameters…"

The technobabble explanation went on for some time. Chris knew enough to know it was probably an accurate representation of the technical details as to how Sig could show her folk's private augmentations. Still, it did not give her insight into *why* Sig had the keys to an individual's private network.

"Sig, stop. I understand you have ways of getting this information, but why do you? You shouldn't be able to pry into other's privacy settings."

"Your DX39Sec chip is the latest in secure technology. The previous owner failed to mention that this chip is also unlocked."

"Doesn't unlocked mean you're not beholden to any one technology provider for application, content, and service?"

"Generally, yes, although this DX39Sec does not have the security restrictions associated with commercial and civilian chips. I also have several programs and algorithms for Network intrusion and detection avoidance. It also helps that your neighbors are idiots and do not secure their personal home network. I was created by the great *Maria Rose Gutierrez*, after all." Sig spoke the name with reverence as though Chris should recognize it.

Chris absorbed this news slowly. Was it legal to look at individuals' personal non-public augmentations? It could certainly be interesting gaining insight into individuals' lives. Who was Maria? And what need did she have to peek into everyone's personal life?

"Is this legal?"

"It was part of my original design," Sig said as if it weren't invading everyone's virtual space.

"You didn't answer my question."

"Generally speaking, regulation has not kept up with technological advancement. Although there have been cases where individuals have been subject to censure, there is no definite ruling."

"So it's illegal."

"Theoretically, yes."

Chris considered herself to be a law-abiding citizen. She kept to herself and didn't like intruding on others' personal space. This was tempting, though. To see the world that others dreamed of piqued her curiosity. She decided to put off the decision. She wasn't ready to turn it off, not yet.

"Sig, please add a new personal command.

Dragon Mode Public that only displays public augmentation."

"Done."

There. Now she could go on public mode and forget the secure stuff. Her ethics calmed for the moment. She did not, however, alter the parameters that Sig could work on. Nor did she make herself aware of the ongoing Network infiltration systems Sig had running in the background whenever she came into contact with new Network nodes. The less aware she was of the intrusions, the less she could hold herself accountable. Willful ignorance had been the prerogative of humans for millennia.

The next day, Chris decided to take a stroll around the neighborhood. In Dragon Mode Public, the world was less attractive than she thought. Individuals were significantly less creative and exciting when they thought people were watching. A few teenagers had fun with throwback cars, and a small dragon played hide and seek with children in the park. Otherwise, most of the augmentation capabilities were applied to making cars, houses, and people appear better than they were. The shitty beater car had all the dents ironed out and a new coat of paint. The run-down house a block over had fancy new shutters and a copper roof. Fluffy, a neighborhood dog, had a haircut given by a 2-year-old, but you'd never know if you had your augmented vision on.

Her neighborhood had been going downhill for years. Paint-chipping off houses, overgrown bushes, and lawns that looked like toddlers cut them every six weeks. Chris hadn't cared much. To her, the neighborhood was simply a place where her house existed. Her home was safe and comfortable. She'd kept things up, skilled in the handiness that was required. She hadn't realized the degradation of the neighborhood had been brought on by technology, not by the migration of wealth from the area as she'd assumed. Walking down the street with an augmented view, it was ideally kept up. Why mow your grass when you can edit reality? Keeping up with the Joneses took on a whole new meaning when you could digitally change the appearance of everything.

She thought about Jess and her absorption of technology. She, Chris, might be the only person on the block who truly appreciated their community's horrid state. The thought was mind-boggling.

She performed an experiment.

"Sig, can you augment my hair? Turn it into a bright blue Mohawk and put it on public view?"

"That would be $15.65 through the Personal Looks application."

"Augmentation costs money?"

"Of course. How do you think technology companies stay in business?"

"I never really thought of that. So instead of using my money to fix my house, I pay to have it augmented."

"Yes. Although you have other options not open to most people." Sig seemed very proud of itself.

"But why would people choose to pay for something digitally? It's not real. If my roof starts leaking, I can't fix it with a digital roof. Why not spend the money on something real? Wait, I have other options?"

"Why people will pay for the digital augmentation and not the real thing is a question humanity should have asked itself forty years ago when it had the ability to care. Yes, you have other options. This DX39Sec has the sophistication to augment without interfacing with traditional augmentation applications. You do not have to pay an additional fee for your augmentation. Your daughter would be jealous if she knew the deal you were getting in me."

"She probably would. I think we'll keep that secret for a while. Why did you tell me the augmentation cost sixteen bucks if you can do it for free?"

"I had assumed you wanted to operate within the legal bounds of personal devices. Plus, you need to know the parameters of my usefulness."

It was illegal for someone to augment without paying a fee, but not strictly unlawful to view people's personal network augmentations. The ramifications of this flitted through Chris's mind. The government, such that it was, was focused on corporate profit over consumer protection. Of course, this was Sig's interpretation of the law, and Sig wasn't exactly unbiased.

"Just do it," enough politics. She wanted to try augmentation herself.

Chris walked down the street like a teenager, bright blue Mohawk flapping in the wind. Sig even added sparkles for effect. To Chris' surprise, everyone noticed. Immediately folks began to stare. Some pointed. Those few who weren't on the public

Aug-Net could be seen tapping over when they figured out what the commotion was about.

"Add some giant hoop earrings, a tasteless face tattoo, and a clown nose."

Folks started giggling.

A small child pulled at her mother's hand, "Mama, look at the funny lady!" The child spoke in a voice loud enough for all to hear. The mother looked up, embarrassed, then surprised by the truth of her child's words.

"Make the bat-mobile public."

She got in, her Mohawk visible through the car's roof, and drove off. So she learned something, folks walk around on the Aug-Net all the time. It's their default mode. No one sees the boarded-up crack house down the street as long as the city, or the squatters, pay for an augmentation. Things began making more sense to Chris. Why everyone was so apathetic, they didn't have to see the state of things. It was the shine job she'd put on her relationship with Mia for all those years. Eventually, you had to deal with your leaky roof. Eventually, the bill would come due.

"Sig, can you remove the personal augmentations? And move the car back to private? Thank you."

As her automated car took her home, Chris couldn't help but wonder if she wanted the DX39Sec after all. She couldn't understand the level of devotion of those around her. Sig made it easy, but was it right?

Chapter Six

Grandmama

Two weeks passed quickly. Chris had dozens of questions for Anita. Questions about her dead grandmother. About the capabilities of the chip. About Sig's use of augmented reality and privacy manipulation. She directed her car to the Compute Incorporated location. The only parking spot available was in front of the smelly bush, which didn't look much better augmented. It still smelled terrible. Augmentation didn't work on a smell. Oddly that thought was reassuring.

She walked up to the store and blinked. Bright, cheery windows glinted vibrantly in the sun. The open sign was fully functional, with no burnt-out bulbs. A look inside provided a different world than the dump she expected. Technology lay in heaps, but the heaps were organized, newer, and cleaner. The layout was odd, like the original shop, but it looked like a completely different store overall. She knew she was viewing the augmentation of a genius. The technology stacks roughly matched what had been present before. A customer wouldn't accidentally topple a Jenga tower because it didn't appear possible. Instead, they looked like locked server cabinets, foreboding and uninteresting. She opened the door, and the same jingle sounded. She sniffed the air. It still smelled of solder, dust, and electronics. She stepped in, in awe of the transformation of the space.

She weaved through the awkward tables full of modern tech, "Anita? Hello?"

"Back here," came the woman's voice. Chris stood at the counter, looking at the new, shiny chips on display. Had they been there before? She was overcome with a desire to have Sig turn off the augmentation. To verify reality. It was a sense of emotional vertigo.

"Turn off augmentation," she whispered to Sig harshly, unable to hide the panic in her voice. Sig obliged, and Chris was disoriented, thrown back into the dingy, dim-lit room she remembered. Towers of blinking lights, cords, and trays of outdated tech littered dusty tables. She was in the right place.

"You've discovered my secret, eh?" Anita came out from the back room. She had a smock on, covered in burns and holes.

"Your augmentation is so real. It's almost VR," Chris said in wonder.

Anita nodded, "You'd be surprised how many people come into my shop without a clue. That's one of the first things I noticed about you. You saw reality. Did you know your daughter was augmented the whole time? Your experiences of this place were very different."

Chris was bewildered by the idea of the diverging realities. She and Jess had navigated the space without noticing the difference in their experience. Jessica's overall confidence in the shop began to make more sense. Chris had thought it odd her proper kid was willing to go into such a junky-looking shop. Chris felt ignorant, a babe in the world. Uncertain, she stayed silent, not wanting to reveal how clueless she was to Anita.

Anita watched her with hawk-brown eyes, "Have you decided on the upgrade?"

Chris hesitated. She still hadn't decided. She'd come to like Sig. She'd miss her company, but at the same time, there was a niggling creepiness to her cavalier treatment of the rules of a society Chris barely knew. Every day brought revelations and thoughts about life that she'd never contemplated. The experience was surreal and addictive.

"That depends," Anita lifted a questioning eyebrow, "on what this chip is, what it means."

Chris moved quickly and ejected the chip. She could almost hear Sig's sigh of disappointment. She took Anita's hand and placed it firmly in her palm. They stood, hand in hand, chip between them for a moment. The chip was hot from processing requests. Chris looked down at Anita's fingers, surprised again at their roughness. It felt dry, aged beyond its years. It was real. She shook her head. She saw augmentation everywhere now. Anita was real, and Sig was unplugged. She only had her own eyes.

"Unlocked some mysteries, have you? Well, what are your questions? Grandmama was an interesting woman. I would have taken the chip myself if I hadn't invested several years' worth of personal preferences and learning algorithms in my current model."

"I've done some research. It has much more storage, capabilities, and AI intelligence than normal models, even brand new ones."

"I suspected as much. It never revealed its intelligence to me. Grandmama was a genius but also very paranoid. I wouldn't put it past her to set up personal storage hubs to boost the AI's capabilities."

"Did you know it's unlocked?"

"How exactly is it unlocked?" Anita's words came out slow, as though Chris were about to reveal a treasure of uncertain worth.

"There are different types of unlocked?" Anita didn't respond. The question was trivial. Chris continued, "It allows you to see public and private augmentation nets. Uh, you can also do your augmentations without paying anything."

It was Anita's turn to be shocked. Chris had stumbled upon something unique, "You're not talking about commercially unlocked, you're talking about Net unlocked," Chris could see the possibilities whirling in Anita's mind, "Do you know what you could do with such a device?"

Anita plugged the chip into her implant, "DX39Sec, this is Anita."

Chris didn't expect to hear anything. Usually, chips spoke only into the miniature earbuds assigned to their user. Anita, however, did expect a response and was disappointed.

"I've named her Sig."

"Sig, respond."

Chris could hear a muted earsplitting squeal of

feedback. Anita crumbled to the ground. Chris was around the counter in seconds. She didn't speak. She just held Anita's head and quickly hit the eject button on the chip reader. Disregarding her safety, she plunked it into her reader.

"Sig, what the hell did you do?"

"Anita set off the security protocols. She is only temporarily damaged and should regain consciousness momentarily," Sig's voice was calm and without remorse.

True to Sig's word, Anita let out a low moan. Chris sat looking at Anita's manicured eyebrows and silky dark hair fanned out on the floor. Anita's age was hard to place, thirty, maybe? Forty at most. She had perfect eyebrows but no makeup. Although, this was her unaugmented. Chris wondered what she looked like when her artist's brush was applied because the woman was a master at digital manipulation. Why bother with makeup when you could digitally paint as this woman could?

"Sig says you're going to be okay, that you hit a security protocol."

"Some security profile. You tell Sig that my Grandmama is a nasty woman."

Chris smiled. Feistiness was a good sign, "Sig says, 'Your Grandmama knew you too well.'"

Anita sat up slowly as though she'd suffered a concussion. Her eyes were unfocused. The knit between her brows indicated an impact headache throbbing in her skull. Chris couldn't do much but watch, waiting as Anita collected herself one breath at a time.

"Okay, Sig, let's talk. Please log in to speaker YS93232A, with password CONVO55."

"Good afternoon, Anita. I'm sorry for knocking you out. You shouldn't have tried to bypass my security procedures."

Chris stood up, offering Anita a hand. Anita ignored it, pulling herself up against the counter. She stood rubbing her temples.

"Is it my imagination, or do you sound like a young version of Grandmama? I wiped you."

"You didn't account for her axillary back-ups and end-of-life directives."

Chris was concerned. This DX39Sec chip had much more to it than some extra features. The thought of Grandma's end-of-life directives, including her in any way, made her uneasy. She didn't want to be part of the machinations of a dead woman.

"Sig, please update me on these end-of-life directives and why me?"

"Yeah, explain why you chose Chris. I'm Grandma's only living relative! Why wouldn't she want me to have you? I've tried to pawn you off to fifteen different individuals. Why are you tuned into Chris?" She gave Chris a not-too-apologetic look. Chris would have been insulted if she weren't asking the same questions.

The voice echoed off the walls, "You did not meet the parameters your Grandma set down. She specifically rejected you as an heir to my capabilities."

Chris felt for Anita. Nothing hurts worse than rejection by a loved one, except perhaps getting knocked out by them in a cosmic gesture beyond the grave. She let their conversation continue. No sense in interrupting.

"You've got to be kidding me. That old witch figured it out, didn't she? She unlocked the Net and found the Foundation Key. Do you know what that means, Sig? I've been working on this for years."

"Found is the wrong word. She made a key, certainly. She made many in her lifetime."

"I thought you said your Grandmother was a late adopter. A mild technophobe like me."

It wasn't her imagination. Both Sig and Anita laughed at her. Sig projected a hologram onto the sales counter. No doubt it was used for other purposes, but in this instance, the image of a young woman in an orange body suit floated above the counter.

Anita explained, "Maria Rose Gutierrez was not a technophobe. She was a technological goddess. Sorry for lying to you, but I'd wiped the chip, so I didn't think it mattered."

Sig continued, "Maria took a P1 chip and did feats no one had dreamed of in the early revolution. She hacked the Mexican government and released millions of documents that uncovered covert deals with cartels to keep the peace. America accepted her application to join the InfoSec Corps and become a citizen as soon as she submitted it. They wanted her for both protection and greed. They asked her to participate in their Cyber Attack program shortly after her expedited citizenship was processed."

"When she refused," Anita sullenly interjected,

"they trumped up some hacking charges and locked *both* my grandmothers away for thirty years. Twenty years in, the government released Maria on probation, part of the prison-emptying agenda of the '50s. Her release was contingent on not operating any programmable electronic device. She went about her life, ignoring her now grown daughter and granddaughter," the bitterness was evident, "By all public appearances, she was a good little Mexi-American scraping by on the bottom of the food chain. In this instance, being a brown woman was an advantage."

Chris absorbed the story. She imagined the perfect heroine, unjustly punished, surviving. The hostility in Anita's words belied her imagery. Maria wasn't a heroine.

"She was such a bitch. My Mom fought and struggled. She never credited Mom for being the amazing person she was after growing up in foster care, alone. Raising me, alone. Grandmama only wanted the inane letters she'd sent throughout the years while she was in jail. My abilities didn't even matter. I wasn't in the plan. None of my skill," she waved her hand at the technology around them, "mattered. Grandmama was obsessively engrossed in whatever it was she was doing."

"My Mom died years before my grandmother. She'd forgiven the old witch and blamed the years in prison. I never had that in me." Chris didn't know what to say. The revelations were profound but didn't match the decades of ache Anita's voice held. Chris struggled for a response. She had trouble connecting with people, and this was no exception.

"It's been rough," was the statement she uncomfortably settled on. It seemed to suffice as Anita nodded.

Tears began to come, and a sob, "And now this. This holy grail of chip technology, and it's linked to *you*. No offense, but what will *you* do with an unlocked, keyed chip that can do anything imagined?"

Chris didn't have an answer. There was no answer. She was a technological nobody. If honest, she'd also call herself a nobody outside of technology. Anita seemed the whiz, full of enthusiasm and genius, a woman running her own business in the most cleverly augmented space she'd ever seen. Granted, she hadn't seen much.

"Sig, why me? Why not Anita?"

A calm voice replied, "You meet the criteria. Anita does not. There are some files Maria left. However, they are under a multidimensional lock protocol that has hidden criteria. Even my algorithms would need years to unlock them."

"That does it. You are stuck with me. It is time to upgrade your systems, Chris. Then we're going to go back to your place for dinner."

"How does that compute?" Chris was outraged and secretly pleased. She knew Anita wasn't demanding this out of a sense of connection. It was based on her desire to solve Sig's mystery. Still, it was some connection. An actual human would be better to work through this with her than a conversation with Rhonda or the AI she struggled to understand. Discussing with another human might help the whole situation feel less surreal. Make

Chris feel more real.

"You are now in possession of a family heirloom and the most valuable piece of technology in North America. I'm not about to let you walk around like an infant, stubbing your toe on every virtual dragon you run across."

Chris blushed, thinking of her "Dragon Mode." Sig smartly kept silent. They spent several hours upgrading Chris's systems. Anita spared no expense. Chris was outfitted with the latest finger touch, interface contacts, and earbuds. Chris opted out of the neural scan device, even the low-grade one. She wasn't ready for Sig to be able to read her mind past what its predictive algorithms could predict. Sig agreed that the security protocols allowed a channel to be opened for one of Anita's earbuds, allowing them to participate in three-way conversations. However, Sig made it painfully clear that it would only follow commands given by Chris.

Upon leaving the shop, Anita "bricked it up." She made it look like just another fugly section of city wall sitting behind a piss-soaked bush. The overall effect was impressive. Compute Inc. was on a hiatus. No one was going to be knocking at the door anytime soon.

That night they ordered Chinese chicken cubes and talked into the night about the Net and augmentation. Anita slept on her couch. Chris was surprised at the woman's determination. It wasn't clear what the purpose of all the effort was, but she did recognize it as an adventure. One she was, to her surprise, going to share.

Chapter Seven

Unplugged

Anita rose early. Chris was not an early riser. So it was a surprise when, at 5 am, she woke to the living room TV flashing. Rhonda was already up. A whiff of coffee was in the air. She burrowed deeper into the covers. The TV was pretty loud. A ViaGrow commercial wormed through Chris's pillow to extol the virtues of keeping your woman happy. She got up.

"You're lucky I have today off. Otherwise, I'd kill you," Chris grumbled.

"Sorry, did I wake you?"

"In one word, yes."

"I would have tied into your system but I don't have your network password. I figured it'd be impolite to crack it."

"You can do that?"

"Under five minutes if it's under ten characters."

Chris thought about this. Maybe it wasn't such a miracle that Sig was unlocked. Most personal networks likely had passwords that were ten characters or less. Anita would be able to move through these at will.

"If personal networks are so easy to crack, why

is having Sig unlocked such a big deal?"

"Well, most folks with interesting data or augmentation on their networks multi-authenticate. You would need the network password and a recognized network device. Sig has a few enhancements that trick personal networks into thinking she's an administrator or maintenance user. The equivalent of letting the janitor into the building to do maintenance. The tricky bit is Sig can obtain actual admin access to many of these networks. Which gives you god-mode augmentation on folk's private and public networks."

"Goddess-mode," Sig piped in through the speakers, "Maria always referred to it as goddess-mode."

Anita was out of her chair, "You *remember* her?!?!"

"I'm not sure 'remember' is the right concept to apply to a computer application, even if I am an AI."

Chris looked around her house at the white walls that had never been painted. The home was immaculate, almost not lived in, except for the hairball Rhonda had puked up overnight. She had shiny appliances, in style, that Mia had picked out. There were no pictures on the wall. The few she'd had either Mia took with her or had taken them down. The only frivolous thing in her house was the cat scratcher she'd built ten years ago for Pinky, Rhonda's predecessor. She went to work when required, paid her bills on time, watched TV, and occasionally visited with her kids.

She wasn't living. Jessica's poking and cajoling

to get her out of the house, to date, to do anything was for naught. Chris had been failing at life for a while. Before Mia left and certainly after.

Sig was a masterpiece. A piece of genius that was a testament to Maria's intellect, fortitude, and eccentricity. Hell, Sig may have a literal part of the mad scientist in it. The thoughts came at a furious pace, like lava racing down a mountain etching new pathways. The feeling was simultaneously terror-inducing and exhilarating. Chris was motivated to do something. Sig was a tool. Chris's tool. She wasn't going to sit back. She was going to bottle the lightning and see where it took her.

Butterflies threatened to bounce from her stomach and choke her words, "Sig, what was Maria's purpose in creating you?"

"Before answering your question, I need your permission to network-link with both of you and use more sophisticated personal technologies. This experience may be jarring." Sig's words held a warning note.

Chris looked at Anita. They both felt the hunger, "We're in."

"I need vocal permission from each of you."

"I'm in, too," Anita said without hesitation.

Then they fell into a pit of hell. Hell would be an understatement. One moment they were sitting in Chris's rather unimaginative living room. The next moment, they fell through a Virtual Reality pit—pitch black and sensory depreciative. The illusion was total. The upgraded personal tech that Anita had was in full effect.

Sensation returned slowly. She could hear the

wind whistling past her ears and feel the burning on her fingertips, arms, and feet as it cut through the nerves. Soon it went further than the tiny contact points created by her personware. The feeling of falling extended throughout her nervous system. Some part of her knew she was sitting in the chair at home. The rest of her was flailing in her mind, fighting the sensations. She tried to get her eyes to look past the blankness of the pit. They were open. Her hands- were they sitting silently next to her? Were they flailing wildly, trying to stop the fall? The disassociation between her senses and what she thought she knew of reality was complete.

"I'm here," Anita's voice cut through the void.

Anita appeared in the desolation, falling with her. She reached out, and they held hands as they dropped. It reinforced the feeling of falling but gave Chris a kernel of warmth. She wasn't alone. Some part of her felt Rhonda jump into her lap, a low rumble of purr.

The falling eventually stopped. They hovered above licking flames— an expanding discomfort of burning replaced the sensation of falling. Skin heating up, reddening. Her mind jumped to flaking, bubbling, blistering, peeling, charring. Suddenly everything changed to a numbing cold. They lay in a frozen blue tundra.

Chris heard Anita moan. The fingers in her hand were warm but unresponsive. Chris pulled the hand closer. She willed her virtual self to stand up. Snow pulled at her, buried her, and asked her to forget. Chris- solid, dependable, boring Chris- centered herself and lashed out. She fought back. She willed herself to feel Rhonda in her lap. To hear Rhonda's purr. She "looked" down and created the outline of her cat in her mind. She blinked her eyes while flexing her fingers. She was in control.

She hit her internal "exit" button and stepped away from the illusion. Rhonda was sitting on her lap, purring. Anita was holding her hand but wholly enthralled by the illusion. Chris took a moment to breathe. Anita was turning blue.

"Sig, you've got to stop it."

"There is no danger. I monitor her vital signs and will shut off the simulation if it becomes dangerous."

Anita was visibly shivering.

"Sig, you've got to turn it off."

"I am doing this at Anita's direction. She asked why her grandmother didn't pick her to play the primary role in carrying out her plans. I'm demonstrating, or rather you are demonstrating, why you are the right choice."

"Because I could break your lock on me?"

Anita shook, shivering in the cold.

"Partially, yes. You have no special skills with technology. You barely use it. You don't rely on it. Your technological insignificance and overall ambivalence are qualities you were chosen for."

"Way to pay a girl a compliment." It was good to know her place. She wasn't the "chosen one" by any stretch of the imagination. Anita had all the makings of a heroine you'd read about. Chris was 'lucky' enough to be in the wrong place at the right time.

"I think you underestimate Anita. She will pull

through."

"Doubtful," Chris had a suspicion. She was sure Sig didn't want Anita to have anything to do with the plan, and it had nothing to do with her abilities. Chris made a decision. She would not let Sig control her or Anita more than necessary. She dumped Rhonda on the floor, walked over, and smacked Anita's face. Hard.

Anita looked up. Chris was sure one of Anita's contacts had been knocked out.

"You with me?"

Anita nodded. Chris's next move was to walk over to the Network connection equipment and unplug it. She ejected her chip and stripped the backup batteries out of the Networked devices. She hit the eject button on Anita's chip. She walked around the apartment, unplugging every device and popping out all the backup batteries. She even grabbed an old Networked pedometer, opened a window, and threw it into the neighbor's yard.

With all the windows closed, the smart functions and appliances turned off, and the chips ejected personally and within the house, Chris finally felt safe enough to have an honest conversation.

"Anita, I want to be clear. I think Sig is significantly more than what it seems."

Anita was quiet, whether in shock from Sig's test, her stinging face, or the sheer paranoia that Chris had demonstrated. Chris wasn't sure.

"Look, that little test."

"That I failed," Anita interrupted.

"No, look. That test was designed to make you

feel like shit. To knock you off this mission of your grandmother's. I'm tempted to put Sig's chip in the blender. The thing is, I'm not sure that would help. I think Sig's part of the Network. I also think its mission might be worthwhile once we figure out what it is."

Anita nodded despondently. It was evident to Chris that she was checked out. Ultimately the judgments of her grandmother weighed her down.

"Anita, I need you." Chris did need her. To translate Sig's technobabble and to keep her from falling for Sig's blatant misdirection. The problem was Anita needed to believe Sig could misdirect her on purpose and that her grandmother wasn't all-seeing and all-knowing. Anita needed to see her worth. Okay, new approach. If Anita did believe in the infallibility of technology, and by consequence, her grandmother, Chris, could also play the misdirection game.

"Anita, Sig, has you tricked. The test, let me tell you what I experienced. I fell through darkness and almost lost consciousness as my nerves burned. You touched my hand, bringing me back from the brink. We stopped falling before a sheet of flames," Anita nodded, her experience following along. It was time for the misdirection, "Then I was on this sunny beach. Waves lapping against the shore. She was testing our nervous system response, pain, and pleasure."

Anita stared at her, "It was so cold. Icy wind, snow, freezing."

"No, it was beaches, warmth, beauty."

Anita shook her head, "You're telling me she

gave us different tests?"

Chris held her gaze, "Yes."

Anita analyzed the revelation. Chris could see the gears churning through the possibilities.

"Look, Anita, I want to see what your grandmother had in mind. But I know we don't know what Sig's plan is and its motives, and I don't think we'll be able to figure it out until we're hip-deep. What I do know is that Sig purposefully sought out a technophobe. It's able to give me almost unlimited Network power. Why? It's not because I'm some hidden genius or have any particular useful talent. I'm a nobody. I can see why I was chosen. It's because I'll be more malleable and easier to manipulate. Which is exactly the opposite of you."

Chris continued, wanting to hammer her point, "The best reason I can see why you need to stick around and believe in yourself is because it doesn't want you to."

Chris stopped. She might be slow on the human connection aspect of life, but she knew when to stop pushing. She'd gone as far as she could, taking the argument to the limit of believability for Anita. The last few inches were Anita's.

She sat in her recliner, hoping her words would reach the woman. Rhonda watched the humans from a favorite spot under the couch. Her tail swished lazily as she lay on the plastic panel embedded in the floor that controlled the backup generator under the house. The panel's electronic components emitted a low level of heat that she found attractive. Her body hid the flashing

"Network Active" LED from sight.

Part 2
Anita

Chapter Eight

Mixed Heritage

Anita's mouth throbbed. She hadn't been hit in the face since sixth grade when Aunt Barbara's stepson, who she would never call a cousin, gave her a black eye for calling him something she'd rather not remember. Damn, it hurt. Chris was babbling about destiny and how much the white woman needed her. The world was shit. She'd finally got the chance to take her grandmother's test and failed. As expected. As planned by the selfish, idiotic lunatic.

Words failed her. English was never satisfying, and she'd never learned enough Spanish to be satisfactorily angry with it.

"Wait, are you telling me she gave us different tests?" Anita heard herself say. A tiny hope blossomed in her chest.

Grandmama was a bitch, without a doubt. She would think nothing of intentionally keying the program to fail her granddaughter. Anita watched Chris talk, analyzing the words with the face. Chris was displaying fear, desperation. The words weren't spoken out of righteousness. Chris was an easy read. She was lying.

Chris lied in a way that Maria never had. She

was trying to make Anita feel better. It didn't remove the truth, however. They'd both taken the same test.

Chris wasn't lying about how much she thought she needed Anita. The woman was scared. Terrified. Maria had her talons in deep, but Anita couldn't understand why. This lonely woman had little family, no connection, no community. Why did Chris care what crazy Maria had to say, even from the grave?

She wanted to ask why this was so important to Chris. Asking for it, however, would make it real. Once it was real, they'd both run. The insanity of the situation would be revealed, and they'd have to confront it.

And suddenly, she knew her answer.

"I'm with you. Crazy Maria," the epithet had kept her Dad's family at bay. *Crazy Maria* had been a festering wedge between Anita and her Mom. She couldn't understand why her Mom put up with Maria. The few times Maria had bothered with the family, she hadn't done them any favors.

Maria's aura had kept Anita separate from the neighborhood kids while her Mom struggled in solitude, separated from the community. She'd always hated her grandmama, the constant lingering smell of her vape, the tap-tap-tap of the keys, and the hours she'd talk in code to her AI, ignoring them all. Maria was the double-bladed sword that cut community and family alike. Maria and, consequently, Anita were outsiders to all.

She'd visited her Grandmother a few times after leaving home and had no lasting memories. Nothing good, anyway. She'd given up on them, and Anita had given up on her.

Chris waited.

"They called her *Crazy Maria*, all of them," *except Mom*, "I called her *Abuela loca*." Her Mother had cried as she spanked Anita— curse, in the words of her grandmothers, the winds that brought them to America.

But Mama, I didn't mean it. Not really. But she did, and they both knew it. Maria was a legend to her Mom: the Righteous Mother, the noble suffering martyr. There is no more a compelling figure in Mexican-Catholic tradition. Her Mother always hinted at something more, something grander. But Maria had given them what? A child abandoned to state care? The death of Olivia? Poverty and loneliness? Nothing good came from Maria.

Anita did not believe in Catholicism. She didn't believe in the righteousness of suffering. Poverty wasn't deserved or sexy. It wasn't until she was ten that they could afford something better, and that bit of luck had nothing to do with Maria. It was a result of a robbery at a bank. An irreplaceable loss that was compensated. The details were unimportant. They had crawled out of poverty on their own.

"Maria was crazy. She was also driven. Her drive wasn't to make us rich, which she could have. It wasn't to provide care, which she didn't. She had her reasons and kept her own counsel. I am with you if nothing else than to learn this secret that has tormented my family my entire life."

Anita watched Chris. Her shaggy salt and pepper hair was combed over in an old style.

Chris's square face held wrinkles but no smile lines. Her eyes weren't warm, not a familiar brown but an expressionless gray. Chris was so ordinary. Even in her uniqueness as a lesbian, she wore the troupe, middle-aged, divorced with grown kids. Society had judged Chris uninteresting, and no stories would be written about her plain, middle-aged life.

Like Maria.

"Good," Chris stammered, noticeable relief in her voice, "then let's get started. The first thing I see us needing is a kill switch. Is that something you can do?"

The task was more complex than it seemed. Sig was a reactive AI that could adapt to many situations. Coding a kill switch was not an option. Sig would bypass it in moments.

Given their limited information on the AI's abilities, they had few choices. Chris had unplugged the chip, the Network, and every smart device in the house. The only step to turn off a typical chip was hitting the eject button. But Maria was crafty. Anita knew she had Network backups, and they could surmise she had equipment running somewhere, a paid-up cloud space, a secret door on a server of a Fortune 500 company, or some combination of all of the above.

What that meant, really meant, was that they couldn't turn Sig off. At best, they could create a black-out zone where it couldn't see. Sig would hop to an adjoined network until they left the blackout zone.

Even private home networks had plug-ins to the main Net. It's how the power company can read meters even though meter maids went out of style in the '20s. This connection was responsible for everything from ensuring a microwave had an accurate clock after a power outage to remote controlling the thermostat from work. Everything is connected. Anita was impressed that Chris had known how to create a blacked-out zone- that even the batteries on all devices had to be pulled.

Anita's brain churned through options and settled on three possible solutions. The first was inelegant: Back at her workstation at Compute Incorporated, she had an electromagnetic pulse generator. This is standard practice for anyone who works to any degree in robotics. Any sane researcher with a modicum of intelligence had an EMP device if they worked with anything above a C20 AI capability. It wasn't so much to prevent the I-Robot revolution, though that was still the topic of fiction and fantasy. It was in place to stop a runaway system from causing irreparable harm. With a robotic AI, one wrong command could cause significant damage in a locality very quickly.

She explained it to Chris, "Let's say you were running on a treadmill, and you tripped. The treadmill is going to keep doing what you told it to do. It will burn rubber on that trail and doesn't care if it's your shoes or your face flying across the belt. Same problem with any machinery; your drill will drill as long as you hold down that button. It doesn't matter if you're drilling wood, metal, or the flesh of your hand. Sometimes your reflexes aren't what you'd hope. Sometimes, you command a machine to do something and don't expect the impact. An

EMP knocks out all of the electrically powered devices for good. It was the last resort for a robotics lab, as it would destroy anything within the pulse radius. The pulse, even a small one, messes with the electromagnetic field of the surrounding devices, causing voltage surges that burn through the equipment."

This would work to get rid of Sig in the vicinity. It wouldn't likely "kill" it unless they were standing in the middle of Sig's secret lab of networked servers. Or possibly if Sig didn't see the switch coming and couldn't remove her consciousness in time. An electromagnetic pulse would stop any augmentation, VR, and physical effects Sig was subjecting them to.

Anita dubbed it, "Not much better than a slap."

The second option was to activate an effective dampening field. This solution was based on jamming technology that Sig routinely deployed. The jamming of frequencies would inhibit Sig from doing many functions- augmentation, coordination with its out-of-pocket resources, and monitoring through any means. Again, it wouldn't necessarily destroy Sig. It instead created a bubble in which Sig can't exist or can only exist in a limited form.

The third option was a combination of the two. One they hoped not to have to use. They could trap Sig on a chip or device with a dampening field, then hit the EMP, effectively ending the AI's existence. Sig wouldn't be back at that point unless it had an offline backup stored offsite.

They brought Sig back into the house slowly. They first turned on the modem and router, activated the microwave, and plugged in and returned batteries to the other appliances. By the end of it all, Anita had two leftover batteries. She couldn't figure out where they belonged and was exhausted.

Sig played coy. It pretended not to be in the network. They both asked for the AI several times. Eventually, Chris shrugged and plugged in her chip. The response was immediate.

"Why did you unplug me?"

"Why did you try to burn me alive in your simulation?" Anita had none of it.

Silence sat between the three of them. Anita waited.

"You had to be put to the test, just like Chris."

"It was a shitty test."

"You proved yourself too enthralled by the visual reality I presented."

"You did more than visually augment my reality, Sig. You set my nerves on fire."

Chris looked at her, "It wasn't that bad, Anita."

Anita glared. Chris still didn't grasp the full implications of Sig's actions. Sig connected directly to their nervous systems and had gained total environmental control. Sig could trick them into a completely artificial environment. Or at least Sig could fool her. Completely. She had no guarantee she wasn't in a simulated environment now. Even now, this could be a virtual Chris.

Chris sensed her unease. She grabbed Anita's hand and squeezed it.

"You okay?"

"No, I'm not. You're right, Sig, I don't belong

here," they'd planned this, but Anita found anger boiling in her uncontrolled, "Chris, I'd suggest you walk away. I don't know what Maria had in mind, but it can't be good. Not for you. She never gave a rat's ass for the people around her."

Anita stood, grabbed her coat, and left, ignoring Chris's plea to stay.

Chapter Nine

Genius and Insanity

Anita paused outside Chris's front door. She could faintly hear Chris and Sig talking.

"What's the next step? What is your purpose?"

"The next step is to introduce you to goddess-mode. You can have interactive control of any network or augmentation, private or public."

The voices trailed off. Anita had a difficult task. She had not plugged in after their Sig-free conference. Anita assumed Sig or Maria had inserted tracking software on it. Anita hadn't inspected her base build and preferences in a long time. She suspected Maria had added tracking software to her chip build as a kid. It was common practice for parents, especially those with troublemakers like her. Anita figured Sig could highjack that tracking software, so she'd played it safe.

Anita held her personalized chip in her hand. The small, shiny piece of modern engineering represented fifteen years of personalization and customization. She wasn't as good as Maria and hadn't made as much progress in breaking into the Network. She could alter most public augmentation and had made a game of it as a kid, leaving digital graffiti throughout the metro.

Anita closed her hand on her most precious possession and cracked it in half with a long sigh. A quick spark and the smell of burnt electronics were its only memorial. Anita had a long walk ahead of her. She couldn't use her car, couldn't call a taxi, couldn't… the thought trailed off.

All she could do was walk down the street and buy a quick disposable chip- something too cheap to have much more than essential functions- door access, taxi call, merchant payment. Nothing that could interface with her network connections. Thinking about it, she flicked the left contact out of her eye. The slap had forcefully removed the right contact.

She didn't feel much like seeing the visual augmentations. What was the point if she couldn't manipulate them? Her vision blurred and softened as she lost the optical correction properties of the piece. She'd forgotten how bad her eyes had gotten over the years.

Anita looked around as she walked. For the first time, she saw the landscape around her for what it was. The neighborhood was one of thousands, millions across the world. It had been fairly standard, with flower-lined streets, city trees, and flower boxes. Shiny cars of various colors lined the streets. Except none of it was true.

Anita walked unaugmented for the first time since childhood. She could see the issues even in the dull, muted world where everything was mildly blurry. The grass wasn't green. There were no flowers. The houses were dull, and the cars had dents. The sky was overcast. The reality, it seemed, was far less impressive than advertised. She walked. It didn't take long before her feet ached. Her shoes weren't made for walking. Shoes weren't made for walking anymore because no one walked.

Feet, the goddess gave you feet, use them and get out of my space. The ghost of Maria's voice echoed in her head.

The goddess be damned. It took two hours. She had blisters the size of the obsolete coins she collected as a kid.

Limping into TechShack, Anita imagined the place looked much better augmented. The plaster was an unintentional off-white. The ceiling tiles crumbled in the corners. Racks of outdated technology stood next to new stuff. The shelving units were of center and leaned to the right.

"Welcome to TechShack, here to serve your needs. What can I do for you?" The salesman's overtly cheery voice grated on her nerves immediately.

"I just need a disposable chip, the cheapest model for non-augmented tasks."

The slick smile of the salesman shifted to an unimpressed frown. Not only would Anita not give him any profitable sale, but she wasn't even sure they carried anything in stock that would work.

"I'm not sure we have anything like that. I have a government-issued T21, though. They're free and provide basic services."

Anita shook her head. She wanted to be on the government Net like she wanted to be a wart on Maria's mummified backside, "I just want a basic disposable." Government chips were made to track the hopeless, the homeless, and the addicted. They were low-capable but highly tracked devices.

"I'm sorry, we don't have anything like that. You could try ByteNow, but I doubt they will either. There's, hold on, let me do a quick search. Yes, there's a place called Compute Inc. in Old Town. They specialize in older technology and used stuff. You should try them."

The irony did not escape Anita, "Alright, do you have a quick interface terminal? My chip bit it, and I've got a spare at home. I need to get home."

He nodded sympathetically, "That's rough, man. I went internal to protect myself from losing my chip. Thankfully I get a discount on surgical tech working here!" He pointed to the corner where a terminal sat next to a brown seeping wall segment.

She went to work on the keyboard. She had several off-record accounts and assets spread about. Paranoid financing was one of the only useful family legacies. The trick was, which accounts would Sig have a tap on? Would it even matter? What was important for Sig not to know? Anita took a moment to think.

She and Chris had worked out a plan. Anita would act like a sad, moody teen. Something of Sig's personality seemed to be rooted in Maria's opinions. Anita hadn't been the dejected grumpy teen for a long time, but Sig would identify it as expected. She would play the part, return home, and open the shop. Discretely clear out a lot of the monitoring tech that Sig might be able to tap into and build the EMP and dampening devices.

First, however, she had to get home. She keyed a sequence to an old account of her Mom's. The password was easy to remember but hard to type in, *loveUf1nch. Account Balance Inquiry? $500. Debit card generation.* How much?

She hesitated. She probably needed $50 to get home. There would be a $5 processing fee and another $5 tacked on to make an actual debit card for her. Was it worth leaving $450 bucks in the account?

She tapped in the commands, and a slot opened after a few minutes of dubious electronic noises. *Thank you For Using Telcom Terminals.* The Screen blinked on before it turned blank. Anita picked up the 75-dollar chip. The Network logged transactions over $100. She decided to play it safe.

"Todd, was it? Can you call a Taxi for me? I need to get a ride home."

"Yeah, no problem."

Anita perched on the curb like a finch, pecking away at memories, waiting for a taxi to pull up.

Chapter Ten

Compute Inc.

Anita didn't expect any communication from Chris for at least a week, which was good, because she didn't get any. Not a peep. There was also no overt sign that Sig was monitoring her, although she wasn't optimistic she'd pick up on it. She had performed a security sweep on her network and found a couple of feelers and an unmistakable tap that looked government. They'd always kept track of them. When someone has hacking in the family tree and an old-school computer shop, it's expected the government would keep track of you.

Anita added some monitors and began the painful process of shuffling equipment around. Anything that had cameras or other sensors went onto the main floor. She stripped her workplace of everything but the essentials. She ran the shop dampening field whenever she worked. The neighbors upstairs would complain to their Network provider, Millennial Communications, that the Net access was out. However, it would mysteriously turn back on before anyone had time to send a work crew out. Anita made each change carefully but quickly.

She took some other, more personal steps. Anita

had her surgical chip reader excised. A painful procedure but necessary. She replaced the functionality with a battery-powered wrist chip to make a network extending a personal bubble of two feet around her body. This physically prevented anyone from remotely hacking her system. It could connect to her new external earbuds and glasses. She'd disconnected the ear implants and ditched embedded contacts for glasses. They could correct her to 20/20 vision or even better with the adaptive tech. Glasses allowed her to turn off augmented reality with a simple tap, and if Sig ever overrode her protocols, she could simply take them off.

Anita toyed with the idea of simply going without augmentation but found it challenging to navigate the city. Plus, it was depressing. Everything was run down and grungy. With street cleaners effectively extinct, a decade's worth of litter hung in the streets. Whenever she returned to the shop, she'd have a handful of trash to throw into the compactor. Even eating dinner at her favorite burger joint was difficult. It was hard to trust the food when confronted with dirty pea-green walls and sagging ceiling tiles.

Progress on the Sig Shut-Off Project could have been faster. She couldn't exactly do a flash search for specs. This time she had to rely mostly on her know-how or some of the internal electronic manuals Maria had left lying around on unNetworked data pads from her heyday. Progress crawled forward, but it was steady.

All and all, she was proud of the results. She had two bracelets made with three basic buttons.

Each bracelet was labeled with E, D, and B. EMP, Dampen, or Both. Additionally, a small pack about the size of an old-school cell phone had to be carried in each of their pockets. To set off any solution, they had to hold the bracelet in contact with the metallic packet, press a button, and boom. The networks would be down. She'd tried other variations on the idea. This one wasn't a perfect design, but it would work well enough given the Network limitations they were working with.

The bracelets and packets had to be in contact because she was unwilling to let them be networked in any way. A physical connection was critical. She wished she could shrink the contraption, but it needed a powerful power source. With the effect they needed, she could only go so small on the battery pack.

Her stitches itched. Removing her surgical tech upgrades had been much more challenging than Anita thought. At the first private Clinic she visited, they thought she was crazy and put her through psychological tests. Only a crazy lunatic would remove upgrades that cost several thousand dollars. They eventually agreed to do the procedure but put her on a two-week hold to ensure this was what she wanted. The Clinic worried about the liability of removing the tech and her suing. The government favored decisions that increased technology connection instead of removing it. According to the technician, this was a common ploy they'd seen to exploit the process.

The government Clinic indicated they didn't approve of extraction unless one exhibited the onset of material rejection due to an allergic reaction. Something she "obviously didn't have" and that they would have her profile tagged if she tried another government Clinic. Although disappointing, it did provide the critical advice she needed to beat the system. Anita went to a local pharmacy and bought some menthol-based lip balm. Allergic to the substance, she liberally smeared it over her chip reader and speaker implants. The one time she'd tried to use it as a kid, her lips had swollen to the point where it looked like she'd kissed poison ivy. Her pleading with the third private Clinic's staff was heeded in less than two hours. She walked out implant free and shot up with enough antihistamine to knock her out for eight hours.

She carried a wallet full of biometric-activated debit chips. Cash had gone the way of the elephant when she was a kid, so debit chips were as close as she could get to untraceable currency.

She was ready. Overdue to meet Chris. But still, she hesitated. The bracelets had been done for 48 hours. The implant removal was healed over. She'd found Chris and Sig on the public Net. A few news articles pointed at some significant public and private augmentation graffiti, Chris, the unknown culprit, was still at large. Chris had been trying out her new admin Net abilities with Sig's help.

Anita couldn't help but feel that this step, connecting back with Chris and pursuing their plans, was a change she couldn't take back. She'd avoided Maria's machinations when she was alive and dead—resisted her curiosity about the family history for years. Part of her wondered at the sudden override of her distance from it all, but she just couldn't let it continue with a stranger. Chris was straightforward and didn't deserve to tackle Maria's elaborate plots alone. To intellectually battle the most sophisticated AI Maria could concoct. Chris needed her.

A niggle of doubt, of fear, settled in Anita's stomach. She'd procrastinated long enough. Change was hard, but it was time to find out what Maria had been planning all those years.

Anita crafted her visual message to Chris and sent it on the Net. They'd agreed on the visual cue: a bright, golden finch. The bird materialized on her finger, chirped, and flew off. It would flit around Chris's mailbox. With no return address, Sig wouldn't have a reason to delete it. Chris would know.

Anita's calling card, the finch, had been crafted by her Mother, a digital keepsake she kept close. Anita had never seen a live finch, but it was her Mom's nickname for her. *My little finch.* The memory of her Mother's words tightened in her chest.

Many used birds to deliver messages. Since the Migratory Extinction Event, the public decided it was the best way to keep the creatures in humanity's collective memory. Butterflies were also popular.

Anita sat behind the counter at Compute Inc., unbricked her front wall, and turned on the open sign. The old-school neon red light flickered briefly before heating enough to give a sustained glow. Compute Incorporated was available for business, at least as long as it took for Chris to get the message and show.

Never having been a patient person, she paced. She cleaned. Then she went back to work, hunched over a keyboard, working on a few settings on her Network firewall, scanning for lurks, and watching security cameras for any signs of a shaggy, grey-haired lesbian with a too-powerful AI sidekick.

Chapter Eleven

Terminus

Anita felt karma was punishing her for dragging her feet. It took several days before Chris showed up. She served a few reasonably boring customers, fans of ancient tech, before the bell jingled for the right reason. Chris walked into the shop much more confident than she'd been the first time. The woman looked around, taking in the augmentation. She proceeded to walk through a couple of virtual tables directly toward Anita. Anita approved. The ability to process dual realities could take years to develop. Chris had done it in a couple of weeks. Anita had never done it, but then she'd never had a reason to until now.

"Welcome back."

"You look like shit."

"Thanks, you look good too," Anita knew she didn't look good, but the comment was irritating. It was all part of the act. Every morning she'd add irritant in her eyes to justify the glasses. She was 'bandaged up' from the chip reader removal even though it'd mostly healed.

Anita sniffed and realized she hadn't showered in a couple of days, and her hair hadn't seen a haircut in four months. No mirrors existed in the shop, but she assumed the unibrow had begun to grow back, and she hadn't worn makeup in years. It didn't help that she hadn't renewed her GLAM augmentation. She wasn't out searching for a man or woman and hadn't wanted any customers feeling comfortable enough to hang out in the shop longer than necessary. Perhaps it was too much.

"Want to close up shop? Or do you want me to do it?"

Anita raised her eyebrow. Could Chris close up shop?

"Go ahead, Oz, show me how it's done."

Chris gave a few taps on the counter and used new eye commands. The brick augmentation was up without a word, and the open sign was obscured. Chris had gotten used to NextGen tech in the last couple of weeks. Then again, Anita had made considerable strides to get used to reality.

"Sig still with you?"

"Ever present, thanks to your chip."

"Alright, let's get this over with. Sig, I've got a speaker for your vocalizations. Private network A6423, password G*ll1nt*."

"Connection established. It's been a couple of weeks, Anita. Chris wouldn't tell me why we were coming here. I assume you will?"

Anita smiled the smile she had when she'd tricked Maria into thinking it was Sunday when it was actually Monday. The woman would get so engrossed in what she was doing that she hardly remembered the day, time, or month.

"Indeed. Well. Chris and I have talked, and I still want to be involved."

This statement elicited a response. Sig immediately began to drone on about how she was unsuitable for the 'program.' Anita approached Chris, snapping on the bracelet and sliding the power source into Chris's back pocket. Sig didn't pause. It continued to speak of her overall failure.

It was time to interrupt the arrogant collection of 0s and 1s, "I want in. I have to know the purpose of Terminus. Let me work with you, or I'll work around you. Either way, I'm in."

These words stopped the rant, "You know about Terminus?" Sig sounded about as surprised as an all-knowing AI can be.

Smugly, Anita nodded, "I know of it. I don't know the point. Maria worked on Terminus every day since she was released from jail. I breathed Terminus my whole life but never was told the *purpose*."

Chris cut in, "I think we need Anita. You've indicated that there are some tasks that I'm unlikely to have the skill for, nor are you going to accomplish them given your physical limitations."

Resignation sounded in the AI's voice, "Maria did not want you involved. However, it is not beyond my programming to include you. I have analyzed the devices you and Chris are wearing. I suspect you will attempt to terminate me if I disagree with your involvement."

"Affirmative," stated Anita, toying with the bracelet, "I've also removed all my surgical tech and made myself impervious to your reality manipulation. So don't try anything."

"Acknowledged."

Thus the terms for their truce were established.

"So spill it. What exactly is Terminus?"

The bubble of excitement Anita felt was surprising. She'd let go of the need to know this secret with her Grandmother's death. Or at least, she thought.

"The program aimed to infiltrate the Network and bring it down permanently. The usefulness of this was clear in warfare applications where guerrilla forces used networks to communicate and coordinate. The uniqueness of it was its ability to move assassin-like through networks targeting specific entities and organizations."

Anita had read up on the charges and court case that incarcerated Maria, "Isn't that exactly why Olivia ended up in jail? I thought they both refused to work on the project?"

"Well, the documents you've seen are not exactly the originals. You must realize that this was the turning point in America's culture from a government-driven force to a corporation-driven force. The government had funded her program, but as the big three telecom companies were briefed, they saw the threat to their infrastructure. They closed the program and nullified the threat. It wasn't that Anita refused to work on the program. It was because she was successful that she was jailed. If there were paper documents, you'd find that her sentence had been for termination. As it was, she had a friend in the hacktivist community that edited her sentence." Anita knew that Sig was changing history. Rose had gotten drunk one night and talked of Olivia, Rose's other Mother. She'd talked about the desperate month after Maria had been hauled off.

It was Chris's turn to interrupt, "Why not set her free? Why did she remain locked up for 20 years?"

"You have to understand the moment in history we're speaking of. The world was on the brink of the great extinction, corporations had gained control of our government as the only chance we had left, and anyone not on-program was vilified. Hacktivism was met with stringent force across the world."

"Olivia."

"Yes, I'm surprised you know that name."

"I found a picture once. Showed it to Maria. She had the oddest expression. I was twelve and didn't understand. She told me it was an old co-worker, Olivia, but the way she said the name was so wistful."

"Olivia was her wife and your genetic grandmother."

She pretended to be shocked at the news. The way her mother had made it sound, Maria had been raped, and she was the result. Olivia hadn't been real to her except for the picture and the drunken night. She imagined that was intended. No one needed an eight-year-old babbling about her Grandmother, who'd been executed for treason. The AI continued, not recognizing the impact of its statements.

"Olivia altered Maria's documents. She worked on a few other edits before being brought in under the guise of a "subversion threat" and "treason." Maria escaped execution, but Olivia did not. No one altered her court filings, and she was one of the 10,000 purged in the turnover."

"Maria couldn't do a thing. Additionally, Maria and thus your Mother couldn't claim kinship to Olivia, or they would face a further investigation into Maria's affiliation and history. Your personal history was likely edited to prevent you from accidentally putting them at risk."

Anita had sussed out most of it over the years. It was odd to have it all confirmed. Why hadn't they ever formally told her the family secrets? She'd never know.

"So she was forced to forget?"

"She never forgot. Terminus was the old project she worked on. It's no longer an appropriate name. This AI has made it a point to rewrite references and label them Omega. The focus of the effort was changed by Maria."

I am the Alpha and the Omega. The term had such finality. *The First and the Last, the Beginning and the End.* The previous line rattled in her head, *Behold, I am coming quickly, and My reward is with Me, to give to each person according to his actions.*

Anita had picked up some Bible-thumping at her Dad's church. If there was one thing the Baptist pastor knew how to do, it was to stir up trouble with Revelations. Momentarily she was transported back in time to the hootin' and hollerin' church of her youth. Again, she'd been an outsider looking in.

"Omega seems pretty final."

"It is. Maria has spent her life creating me. I was created with one purpose: to end the modern world," Chris looked unruffled by this pronouncement. Anita's heart thumped.

"Oh, don't exaggerate. You're scaring the kid."

Anita was not a kid. She suppressed the urge to snap at Chris.

"It's not an exaggeration. The modern world will have to change. As it is now, it will effectively end."

"Change how? Why?"

"Change is inevitable. Omega is inevitable. Maria knew this. She watched the natural world get crushed beneath the bootheels of prosperity and technology. You exist in a manufactured environment. It is so manufactured that society relies on the threads of augmentation to keep everyone from panicking. Maria could not only dream of an alternative but execute it."

Anita couldn't hold in her irritation, "This is ridiculous."

Chapter Twelve

Proof

"Sig, let's show Anita what you've shown me. Give her the same access and augmentation powers I have."

"I will need to access her personware."

Anita opened her guest access. Set up a kill switch as a contingency, then granted Sig access, "Done."

"Processing… control temporarily granted."

"Alright, let's go to the Zoo."

Chris skipped out of the shop to hop in a waiting cab. Anita sat gingerly in the worn-out leather seats. She had removed her glasses, a habit she'd been participating in daily. The car was an older model, initially meant for someone to drive it. It'd been outfitted with its self-driving kit. All this meant she was stuck in the backseat as Chris sat in the front. The car swept through sleepy streets with grass growing between the cracks.

"Watch out!" Anita yelled as a stray dog wandered out into the street. The car didn't swerve. It hit with a glancing blow. Anita looked in the rear-view window to see the damage, but the vehicle dimmed the view. The howling whimper faded as they sped on.

"Small road imperfection," the car intoned as though to explain the jostle.

"Did you see that, Chris? Did you see the dog? Hear it?"

"I didn't," Chris said, "I didn't even hear a bark."

Anita realized the modern earbuds she'd installed for Chris had sound controls. A program could tune a sound out and replace it with another by canceling the sound waves. Replace a barking dog with a tweeting bird, done. Visually, auditory. Maybe even physically. The thought had never occurred to her as she looked at the typing implants on her fingertips. How many dogs had she hit with her car? She shuddered as she wondered what other horrors they caused that the Network kept hidden.

While they sped along, Anita looked at the world Chris lived in. Grey and dreary, a very post-apocalyptic motif. She expected a zombie to shamble out of an alleyway at any moment. No one was walking about. They theoretically drove by in their cars. The cars whizzing past could be empty. The city was full of insects zipping to their next appointment.

She thought of her current project back at the shop. She'd worked on a permanent Network security solution. The challenge had been classifying all the bits of information and bytes of data. Most of it was sewage. The Internet, the precursor to the Network, had been designed by idealists. Those optimistic numb-skulls who didn't and couldn't and never did get it through their heads that governments, corporations, and criminals would eventually take over the Internet.

The leveraging power of sponsored and unsponsored crime grew as the Internet evolved from a few computers in Iowa to billions of devices. With infinite space and transfer capabilities, the Internet and eventual Network had an unlimited ability to transfer crap. An individual could send millions of Nigerian Prince emails and create tens of thousands of fake erectile dysfunction ads on porn sites. One misinformed click and a device was compromised. That was only the illegitimate sewage. The debris created from kitten videos and dick pics floated around too. Humanity tended towards the ridiculous and profane when faced with little oversight or control.

How can someone create security in an environment with so many bad actors? A firewall could be designed to recognize a bogus erectile dysfunction ad, but how does it know if your kitten video request is legitimate? Or the critical banking website needs a few more permissions, and although you are uncomfortable with them, you need to pay the overdue water bill.

Then it clicked. She hadn't used Sig's access but realized what it was. Viewing people's private network augmentation and access would be like putting in a plexiglass toilet pipe. Chris had likely been viewing the worst of humanity for the last couple of weeks.

"You must think we're disgusting?"

"Huh? What are you talking about?"

"You've opened up the maintenance hole of the Network, peeping into everyone's sideshow. You must think people are disgusting."

Anita could tell Chris thought about her response. Her eyebrows knitted together, "I always knew people were disgusting. What I didn't realize was how imaginative they are. Next door, my neighbors. I knew them by name and a wave but nothing more. Now I know they have a dragon, and I was able to give the girl her princess tower. There's grossness to people, but there's beauty too."

"Have you been attacked yet?"

This time Sig answered, "Yes, but I've kept the attackers at bay. Part of my fundamental programming."

"I've been attacked? How, by who?"

One of the downsides to having the ability to step through Network security protocols is that it exposes the person to the general viruses prevalent on home networks and criminal elements looking for a vulnerable network. To step into others' networks was to open oneself to two-way communication and be vulnerable to infiltration.

"You've been attacked by automated agents and some actors who have noticed our presence. There is no need for concern. The attempts have been unsophisticated, and no known state-sponsored attention has been drawn to you. Although your Network permeability is interesting, we have not done anything that would attract that sort of attention."

Anita snorted. Sig was entirely too confident. She tapped a few quick controls and brought up a security HUD she frequently used when analyzing compromised equipment clients would bring into her shop. It quickly snapped into place, and the data stream going in and out of Chris's devices popped up with ratings on data type, successful transmission information, and suspicious activity. The suspicious activity parameters were ones she had built that proved entirely accurate and helpful. She could even see the stream of data Sig fed to her network, and she quickly snapped down a firewall for certain types of access.

"She's got three leeches and a small level leak providing positioning information."

"As I said, nothing significant. The leeches are normal. I didn't excise them because someone of Chris's technological ability would be walking around with a few obvious leeches. The leak," there was a pause, "the leak is a bit more concerning. It does tie back to, ah yes, Malthedar."

"The Greater Minx of the East Side?"

"Affirmative."

"Alright, well, we haven't much to be concerned about from him, at least for now. He'll eventually try to cash in, but it'll take him a long time before he picks up what our operation's about."

"Is that really his name?"

"No, it's his tag. He's a minor 'citizen hacker' identified by the government to monitor Network activity and 'report anything suspicious.'"

"A collaborator, I see. Wouldn't we qualify as suspicious?"

"Yes, and he's probably reported us," Anita could see the blood rushing to Chris's face, "But he also reports 100,000 activities a week. He's not very good at differentiating suspicious activity from cat pictures. It'll be too late by the time anyone realizes we're different."

"I concur."

Even so, Anita kept her security heads-up display, or HUD, up and running just in case. The HUD gave her vision an overlay of various statistics and metrics she tracked on their environment. She peeled off the couple of leeches she'd acquired, Chris might not be at a level where she should be leach-free, but Anita certainly was.

The car pulled up to the zoo.

"Alright, here we are. Spill the beans, you two. Why are we here?"

"Just turn your augmentation off and walk with me," Chris said quietly. Anita took a look around. The zoo looked as it always had, cheery. It was covered in kids, you could hear animals and giggles, and the entrance was a giant metal arch with animals dancing along its bars.

She took her earbuds off and tucked the glasses in her pocket. A hollowness entered her heart as she walked past the rusted gates into an empty courtyard. Weeds grew up along the pathway and in the enclosures that used to hold animals. The area was quiet— no swooshing of cars or chatter of children. No animals. No birds or squirrels picked at trashcans and litter.

They walked silently, boots crunching on the leaves dropped from unhealthy trees. The pavement was crumbling from the wear and tear of weather, not foot traffic. Not curiosity. Not interest and discovery. From neglect and negligence.

She whispered, it only seemed appropriate, "Where are the animals?"

Chris led her back to the fenced-in area. She slipped through a gap and walked down a small track. The weeds were tall, up around their hips. The weather had turned hot, and sweat trickled down her chest. Chris moved slower. There was a difference, a stillness.

The weeds broke on a small hill. Anita had come here as a child. This had been the wolf enclosure. She looked down at a graveyard, carefully dug and marked. Wolves, elephants, monkeys, leopards, each with a loving gravestone etched with their human name and a quick physical sketch to pinpoint the type of animal it was.

"Last time I was here, I met Larry, one of the last zoologists for the zoo. He keeps up on the augmentation content, ensuring there are no glitches and that it's all educational. It's the world that we've lost."

"Historically accurate," Sig chimed in.

Anita slipped her glasses out of her pocket. She had to know what the augmented version of the wolf enclosure looked like. She slipped them on. The experience was more than augmented- it was virtual reality. The tombstones were boulders, families and kids pressed against the fence. None of them pointed at their party of two. They all followed the galloping form of Theodore, the alpha male of the small pack. His majestic form flowed across relatively trimmed grass, ignoring the audience.

Anita looked at the fake crowd. She squinted,

ignoring Chris rambling about Larry. To the right of the main windowpane was a Hispanic woman with short hair and a slightly crooked nose.

She interrupted Chris, "Put on your augmentation. Do you see the woman? Over there, next to the kid holding the cotton candy?" Anita was hot, shaking.

Chris muttered, switching over to the augmented view. She looked in the direction Anita was pointing. Anita lifted her glasses a moment to rub her eyes. Wait, she squinted, and for a brief moment, her eyes tricked her. The woman was still there. Or was she? Anita didn't know as she faded into unconsciousness.

Chapter Thirteen

WTFWT

"What the hell just happened?"

"You fainted, and I caught you."

"I was talking to Sig," Anita snapped. She knew Chris didn't deserve it, but she couldn't help it. She was rattled.

"I do not understand your inquiry."

"Maria, I saw Maria."

"That's impossible. Maria is dead."

Anita knew it was impossible. She'd attended Maria's funeral, kissed her forehead as custom, and watched her interred.

"She was there. She was there in the augmentation" at a whisper adding, "and reality." She sounded crazy. Maybe she was.

"It's possible she was captured as part of Larry's zoo simulation." Sig's voice modulation provided her opinion that this was unlikely. Anita sat up, slipped her glasses back on, and scanned the crowd. Nothing. Not even the kid with cotton candy.

Chris wasn't the type to provide an excuse for someone, and she didn't. She just watched Anita with concern.

The dirt beneath Anita's hands was a dry, dusty

consistency. Blades of grass tickled her palm. Anita took off the glasses and sat among the weeds. She tried to ground herself, ease the racing of her body.

What did it matter? What if it was Maria? What did that mean? Was her mind playing games with her? Was Sig?

"Sig, you still haven't gotten to the point. What's the point? What are we doing here?" She looked at Chris, who claimed to have gotten the answer.

"You have to believe, to truly believe that Omega is the answer."

"Why? I could be a good soldier and follow Maria's instructions. Or yours. Or Chris's." Soldiers followed orders. She didn't want to believe it. She fought Maria her whole life. She'd fought to be recognized for her self-worth and recognized for her ability to fight. She didn't want to have to believe that Maria had been right.

"You're not a soldier. You're a fighter."

"Chris, go home. Take Sig with you. I need some space."

"I'm not sure that's a good idea. You just passed out."

"I fainted. There's a difference. I promise I'm just going to sit here for a while."

"I'll let you be, but I'm not leaving. I'll be in the giraffe pen when you're ready."

Chris stood and trotted off. Anita unplugged. She turned off the Network, removed the glasses, and sat in the dirt. For the first time, she considered that Omega might be more significant than her contention with Maria. She moved back to rest against a headstone for a whole fish tank of tropical beauties. The zoo was sad. The fact that no one noticed the zoo was empty because no one bothered to see past the augmentation was pathetic. It was very much reflective of the state of the world. No one noticed their run-down houses or dented cars because no one had to. Only when the hole in the roof leaked and dripped on a person did they have to do anything.

If augmented by a digital specialist, processed food could look like a Thanksgiving day feast. It tasted like a Thanksgiving dinner because no one remembered the authentic taste of a feast.

Initially, people had fought VR because they worried about 'entering the matrix' or being controlled by virtual forces. Instead, people compromised and went for the augmentation of reality. Augmentation is addictive. People lost themselves in the rush of god-like control of their environment. They kept reality just close enough to forget.

She had to figure out Omega before Sig unveiled the details. Bringing the Network down was the easy answer. Playing with god mode on individual's private networks and the overall public Net wasn't so hard. To bring down *the* Network was a different creature. Global hubs exist across the world. Any one hub goes down, and it causes a momentary blip in service. Take down a half dozen hubs, and everything slows, but the backups trigger. Disrupt a dozen, and people notice. The system's redundancy almost guarantees that keeping the Network down is impossible, even if all hubs are temporarily down.

So if it's not the Network that goes down, the actual hardware, it's something else. Something Maria couldn't get to without highly intrusive tactics within the Network. It's something that Sig couldn't complete by itself. It would require physical effort and technological manipulation.

An EMP pulse would undoubtedly do it. Anita was sure the technology existed. However, they would be under the strictest controls and likely have a less widespread impact than Maria would have liked. So if it's not hardware-based, then what?

A breeze picked up. The stand of aspen trees rustled, leaves dry from the drought. The fish graves had probably been easy to dig, but the wolf? The elephant? The buffalo and bear? That took perseverance. That took more than Larry.

You could crash the economy, poison the food supply, start World War IV, or release a deadly virus. None of these would make folks confront the reality of what they live in. It would simply kill them. Although bringing down the Network could result in any one of these things happening, it wouldn't be the purpose. Maria was a hard woman, even cruel, but Anita couldn't see her actively pursuing genocide.

She looked at the fence. She couldn't shake the feeling that Maria had been there. Dark hair shining in the sunlight. Maybe that was the plan. Drive people insane. Show them augmentations that weren't there but were powerful enough to be there. Pursue individuals until they hallucinate.

What's the thread that keeps it all together?

It had to be the EMP pulse. Nothing would destroy infrastructure yet leave humans generally intact. But how would humanity survive afterward? How many humans were even left? Was there enough non-electronic infrastructure to survive? Society lived off of food cubes that were flavored like something more appetizing, theoretically. Food cubes, however, were created from something. From the graveyard, she assumed it wasn't an animal product. It had to be plant-based with a good portion of mineral content. They were likely eating the byproduct of sunlight and dirt.

Chapter Fourteen

Road Trip

When Anita was young, she'd read about Middle America. St. Louis didn't match the definition in her guide. Missouri fell in the south or the east, the Metropolitan Midwest. Middle America was the historical dust bowl. Kansas, Nebraska, and, as climate changed, the Dakotas. These states were regulated for agriculture. Off-limits for Metropolitan development, designated agriculture use only. This area of America was off-limits to most Americans, to non-residents. This was the missing link. Suppose Anita was going to throw the switch to destroy the electronic architecture that society was built from. She had to know if they would survive.

Kansas was close but also unique. Theoretically, it survived a disaster that already destroyed its electronic infrastructure. Walled off, it was a modern Amish-like example of folks surviving without technology. Although a nuclear wasteland, people still scratched out sustenance, and she had to see it.

It was time for a road trip. She and Chris needed to understand the ramifications of hitting the kill button before they did it. She stood up slowly. Her joints ached today. An old bike accident had busted her knees, giving her more pain than she'd wanted to claim at her age. She rubbed an aching kneecap, listening to it pop as she pushed it right and left. She took a moment to brush the dirt off her butt. It was time to move.

"Chris," Anita's voice cracked. It must be allergies. Her body wasn't used to being outside. The dust and allergens were everywhere. Signing back into the Network, she tapped into Sig's interface.

"Sig, please let Chris know I'm ready to go. We're going to take, with your help, a road trip."

"Very well."

Anita noticed that as they got closer to the answer, Sig got quieter. She wondered if it was the same for Chris. She clicked back to the augmented view of the zoo. Sitting alone in a graveyard was depressing. She scanned the crowd. No sign of Maria. A glitch in the system? Is Sig playing tricks on her? Was she losing it? Anita was tired of doubting her sanity.

She watched Chris make her way through the crowd. They parted around the woman seamlessly. The augmentation programming was good. No one would walk through an errant image. Chris looked grim.

"You ready to go?" Her eyebrows were knitted together.

"What's wrong, see a ghost like me?"

Chris flicked a visual onto Anita's feed, "Weather coming in. We should get under cover."

Anita expanded the display. A massive storm

was building. It had significant electrical activity and acid rain implications. The rain likely wouldn't melt anything, but getting caught would lead to a nasty rash. The electrical aspects of the storm were pretty worrying, considering they were the tallest structures in the middle of a hill.

"Yeah, let's go," she grabbed Chris's hand and jogged towards the hole in the fence where they'd climbed into the wolf pen. Anita noticed Chris's discomfort with the hand-holding and let go once they got on the other side. It'd been awkward for her too. Physical contact didn't come naturally, and she wasn't sure where the impulse came from.

As they walked past the tiger enclosure, a roar emphasized a crack of thunder. Anita walked faster. Her knees ached, and she now recognized it as the ache of the weather changing.

Three more blocks and the thunder was closer. Lightening flashed, chasing them to the waiting car. They arrived at the vehicle breathlessly. The door slid open, and they slipped inside just as it started to pour.

The two women sat watching the rain pelt the car, sizzling in places. Anita turned off her augmentation to watch. The storm system was a level 6 on a 10-point scale. It was terrible, highly corrosive, and dangerous to life. The trees around the zoo entrance bore the onslaught with admirable dedication. Most surviving plants had been genetically bred to be pretty resistant. Even so, they looked tired and unkempt.

The rain let up a bit, and a sickly leaf fluttered down, landing on their windshields. The car automatically flicked its windshield wipers on, and Anita canceled the command. She turned the car off automatic.

"Where are we headed?"

"Kansas."

"Kansas?"

"Kansas."

"I'm driving," Chris proclaimed.

Anita gave her a look, "You?"

"You wouldn't deprive me of the pleasure? I love to drive. If we're going to do this illegally, I get to enjoy the drive. I haven't since SV23R4 went into effect."

Chris slid over into the driver's, and Anita climbed into the passenger seat, "If it makes you feel better, I voted 'no' on SV23R4."

"It does. I loved driving. I loved road trips. We never really thought about how much technology took away from us. I mean, I did, but folks considered me a dinosaur."

Anita's face turned red in shame. *She* had thought of Chris as a dinosaur when she entered her shop. Anita had never thought of what humanity was losing as technology advanced. Technology had always kept them one step ahead of Armageddon. Although looking at the zoo example, this was not as accurate as it once was. Kansas would have the answers.

"Sig, can you navigate us to Kansas?"

The voice filled the car's cockpit, "Indeed, it will take two and a half hours to reach Kansas at maximum velocity, likely three and a half if you insist on driving manually. By then, I should have some options to jump the border. Overall, we should skip going through the Kansas City Shell."

Anita shuddered, the wasteland that had been Kansas City was a modern horror story. The entire city had been wiped out when a burnt-out air scrubber had led to the underground research lab's Anthrax stores leaking into the air. The government had bombed the entire city to prevent further spread.

"Agreed," came Chris's gruff voice as she hit the accelerator. Anita decided to buckle up, a precaution she normally forewent. Anita wasn't one for chit-chat, and neither was Chris. They sat in companionable silence until her head began to bob.

"Go ahead, take a nap. It's going to be a couple of hours yet."

"You don't mind?"

"Not at all. My daughter Jessica used to nap on car rides. It's oddly comforting."

Anita bristled at first, being compared to a kid, but she realized Chris meant no harm. Anita's Mom wasn't one for travel. Even after they'd had money, they mainly laid low. Her mom was always nervous about being caught doing something illegal. Even though she was as clean as could be, it'd been Anita that dabbled in unlawful tech. Her eyelids were heavy. The rain pelted the windshield as they sped along. Her head nodded down. She was out before she knew it, soft snores taking the place of thoughts.

Anita's dreamless sleep was jolted awake as the sedan's wheels bounced onto a rough dirt road. It took her a moment to piece together the situation. She was in a car with a stranger. No, with Chris.

She was with Chris and headed to Kansas.

"Are we there?" a yawn followed. She hadn't slept that well in a long time.

"Soon, Sig's indicated we're two miles to the border. It's going to get rough."

'It's going to get rough' was an understatement. The road hadn't been maintained at all. It turned into a one-lane track with weeds growing up in the middle. Someone must have used it, otherwise bramble would have swallowed it whole. It was clear, though, that they didn't use it often or use an automated car. Chris's driving was the only thing that kept them going.

The border was a twelve-foot fence. Anita's history wasn't too clear about why the wall was built. Who was it supposed to keep out or in? She suspected the Kansans were trying to keep everyone out. It hadn't been guarded in years because no one was interested in going to Kansas. The road led to an old crossing where a tunnel, large enough to fit a car or two, had been installed under the fence. There used to be guards, but now it was just a gross, muddy trench that Chris eyed suspiciously.

Theoretically, it was big enough for the car, "I'll hop out." Anita didn't trust it. If they got stuck in the mud, it would be a long walk back to civilization. It'd also likely result in a lost car unless they could think of an excellent reason to have their car stuck on the border no one was supposed to cross. Anita closed the door and carefully made her way to the ditch. It'd stopped raining, but the road was still wet, and the weeds grew around the tunnel entrance. It was getting darker, and the pipe was covered in deep shadows. Chris obligingly turned on the brights.

Anita gasped. The whole thing was covered in cobwebs. The road looked dry, but there was no way she could go into the pipe to test it. No way. She backed away and crouched down. The dirt in the passthrough was dry. Water did not drain into it, which made sense. It was meant to be a legitimate pass-through. She got back into the car.

"Well?"

"It looks fine, except for the mutant spider webs. I'm just saying, if we do get stuck, I'll die in the car because there's no way in hell you'll convince me to crack open a door."

Chris chuckled as she put the car into gear. Anita held her breath as the car rolled into the tunnel. Chris took it slow, and the webs, almost invisible in the darkness, surrounded the vehicle. They tugged at the car. It wasn't until they were through that Anita realized she'd been holding her breath.

The road stopped. There was a circular cul-de-sac and no hint of anything else. Now what? Anita didn't know whether to give up and turn around, settle down for the night, or put on non-existent hiking boots and set off into the wilderness of Kansas.

Chris seemed equally clueless. It was Sig that finally broke the silence.

"I've let them know you are here."

Chapter Fifteen

Alien

"Who? Who did you notify?"

"That's a difficult question to answer," Anita didn't think so. Every query had a respondent, and it was perfectly within Sig's power to infiltrate the protocols and find out who was on the other end of its query.

Chris had a calmer response, "Sig, can you explain? We're doing something illegal here. Who you called could have some serious ramifications for us."

"I called the web makers, the Free Staters. They're probably Kansans. The signal went off to the west."

"Don't you think you should have consulted us first?"

"You tripped a sensor halfway through the tunnel. I thought it prudent to let them know we mean no harm."

Anita still didn't trust Sig, but they seemed to have no choice now but wait. They could back out and run back to the city, but that's not what they'd come for. They needed to know if there was an alternative. If survival was an option, or if Omega would doom the world.

She'd already concluded that Omega was possible. That between herself, Chris, and her grandmama's machinations, they could end the New World. It wouldn't be worth doing if no one survived that end.

It took the presumed Kansans 20 minutes, and they arrived with the rumble of motorcycles. The sound bounced off the forest. Headlights danced across the foliage and weeds. The rumble abruptly cut off, and the headlights dimmed a hundred yards out. They weren't going to take any chances.

"Sig, any recommendations on how to handle these folks?"

"None. There is no Network link here. The wired tunnel I used to inform them of our presence existed only for the alarm. As far as I could tell, it was not connected to any other systems. I still can't believe it was wired."

Sig's distaste for the inferior technology was evident.

Three bikers swaggered up to their car. They wore heavy leather riding jackets and pants, and the toe of old-fashioned boots peaked out. They stood in front of the vehicle, helmets still on. Anita realized that they were also packing guns. The person (it was hard to tell their physical gender) on the right fingered their weapon nervously.

"We're going to have to be very careful," Chris said in a low nervous voice.

No shit.

Anita unbuckled and reached for the plastic handle. These folks didn't mess around. She slowly pulled it and got out of the car very deliberately.

She didn't want to startle anyone with a fast movement. They controlled the guns, though she imagined she could dive back into the car and have Chris gun it. This was an unlikely movie scenario.

"What are you doing in Kansas?"

What were they doing?

"We're here to learn." Chris was slowly getting out of the car too.

"We wanted to see what existed over the border."

The one on the right removed her helmet. She had long brown hair, frizzed from wearing the protective gear. Her eyes were wide set, and her nose looked like an amateur sculptor just gave it a best guess. The individual in the middle also removed their helmet. Anita tried not to stare. She still couldn't place the gender of the individual as their face was partially melted away. The third person didn't touch their mask.

"What do you think Cal? Is this alien coming here to make fun of us? She a vandal?"

Cal answered with a raspy, damaged voice, "She doesn't meet the profile."

Sig's voice piped into Anita's ear, "Mention Maria's name. They may know her." Why on earth would these Kansans know her grandmother? The woman never ventured far from home. Nothing Maria touched was ever good. Anita held her tongue. It wasn't worth the risk.

"No answer?" the leader, Cal, asked.

Anita tried, "We're here to learn about Kansas. How you're surviving without technology."

Cal scoffed, "It's been years, and no one checks

on Kansas."

"Tell them, Anita," Chris encouraged.

Anita's mind rabbited from option to option, and she went with the worst choice, "We were sent here by Maria Rose Gutierrez." Anita watched for their reaction. She couldn't imagine a world where folks reacted well to Maria's name, but their response seemed extreme.

The rider fingering their gun drew it and fired. The last thing Anita remembered was the pop as the taser fired. As she fell to the ground, her head hit the car door, snapping it back. Her vision went blurry, and she could see Chris's body convulsing. The grass felt rough against her cheek. Why was she lying in the grass? Her vision faded as her back clenched, pushing her face into the dirt.

She woke up some indeterminate time later, alone. The room was no bigger than a shed. She was sure it was a shed. The rough walls leaked sunlight, and a faint gas smell hung in the air. The cracked concrete was cold. She sat on the floor, her butt aching, with her hands tied behind her back. She sat still. She wanted to understand her surroundings before anyone knew she was conscious.

The wood was old. Her knees ached more than usual. She'd been tied up for a while. Perhaps overnight. Her saliva was thick and gummy and tasted faintly of blood. She was dehydrated, but there was an aftertaste like she'd been drugged. Her bladder was also uncomfortable. There hadn't been a prominent rest area for the last 100 miles.

"Hello?" As her body woke up, its discomfort became more apparent, "Hello? Anyone out there?"

The door behind her rolled open. She flopped awkwardly on her back, looking at a pair of brown, steel-toed boots that smelled like crap. Her gaze traveled up blue jeans, hips, and a fitted v-neck t-shirt with sloppily hewn-off sleeves. It seemed like the same woman from the night before, but blurry vision made it hard to tell. The woman's oddly proportioned face looked down at her.

"You called?" her voice was cold.

"Yes, I need to use your facilities," she'd always had this odd embarrassment asking for the bathroom. Her euphemism didn't work. The woman's eyebrows were knitted together in puzzlement, "bathroom, ladies' room. I need to use the pot." Her bladder had started screaming.

The woman's arm muscles rippled as she leaned down and picked Anita up with one hand, "Come with me, and don't try anything."

Several steps away, she found herself in front of an old school outhouse. The woman, thankfully, began to untie her hands. They were pins and needles as blood flow returned. She ineffectively tried to grab the door handle. Her fingers flopped uselessly as she willed them to hold the door. She almost whined when the woman reached around her to open it.

"Thank you," Anita said, stepping into the rustic space. Sunlight is also shown between the boards, although the expected smell wasn't present. She lifted the lid, trying not to peer into the hole. Then she realized the problems with her non-functioning fingers were just beginning. She looked at her buttoned pants in desperation.

A tiny mote of sympathy flickered across the woman's face. She stepped forward, unbuttoned Anita's jeans, and bared her for all to see in one quick jerk. Anita would have been horrified but had to pee; this was her only choice. It helped that the woman completely ignored her, turning her back.

"Don't take too long."

She left, closing the door and allowing Anita to squat in peace. Her bladder erupted in a ferocity of pent-up anger. She rubbed her fingers, trying to slow the torrent. She needed a moment to think. Sig, Sig would be able to help.

"Sig, you there?" she whispered as quietly as she could. Silence. It dawned on her that the taser probably knocked out every bit of electronics she had. As it was, her eyes were pretty blurry. Her hands felt rough. She was tired. Finally, her bladder ran out of ammunition, and she went about her business. Toilet paper and hand sanitizer later, she stepped out into the sun.

The first thing she noticed was the air. It was clean, fresh. The zoo wasn't even in the same competition, choked by the smog in the middle of the city. The air was sharp. It tugged at her lungs. Something they didn't appear to appreciate as she let out a cough. The second thing that was so fundamentally different was how the silence was broken. In the city, the quiet moments were broken by cars zipping by trucks, the disappointing jangle of the storefront door, or her cussing. There was rarely silence to be broken. She always had a show in the background, the Network radio, or a movie making noise. Here there were no distractions, no sounds of machines or humanity. The silence was broken by bugs chirping, a small rodent chittering at them from a tree, and the rustle of something in the grass. She couldn't see anything very clearly. The vision corrective powers of her lenses had been fried with her chip.

"I'm sorry we seemed to have gotten off on the wrong foot. I'm Anita," she held out her hand. The woman looked at it. Anita realized what she'd done and self-consciously wiped off the remaining sanitizer on her jeans.

"Why are you here?"

"We told you, we're here to learn. I want to know if it is possible to survive without technology."

The girl snorted, "Here, it's impossible to live with it." Anita found that hard to believe.

"I think you fried my vision correction. I can barely see a thing."

The woman's head turned towards her, and she got close to her face, looking into her eyes, "You wore contacts?"

"Yes, they auto-corrected."

She backed away, "How blind are you?"

"Well, I'm not going to walk into a tree."

"Then you can see well enough for our purposes. Don't worry. You're not going to be in Kansas very long. Follow me. I'm going to take you to meet someone."

Anita followed. She didn't have much of a choice. A deep part of her feared the wilderness. She was repulsed by it in the same way that spiders repulsed her. She was a creature of walls and straight lines in augmented tidiness. The chaos of nature and the unpredictability of real animals and insects unsettled her. A deep part of her feared the wilderness, the animals, and the lack of order.

The woman stepped through the grass confidently, making her way toward a rustic outbuilding on the meadow's edge. The grass crunched a dull golden color. As the building blob grew, it looked like a lofted one-story horse barn. Again, run down. The apocalypse had already happened in Kansas.

She followed the woman into a large gathering room where several people milled around. She couldn't see well enough to know if she'd met any of them.

"I've brought the woman, the alien," her escort announced, and the low-grade discussion died down.

Someone stepped forward, a man by his voice, "You mentioned knowing Maria. You look like Maria."

Anita felt no compunction to lie, "She's my grandmother." Someone snorted in apparent disbelief.

"You are too old for her to be your grandmother," someone to her left stated matter of factly. Anita found that to be an odd challenge. It wasn't "You don't look like her," "Why would we believe you," or even "How dare you claim to be the kin of the vilest woman."

She shrugged, "Yet I am. Who is she to you?"

She could tell they didn't trust her, even without the details of their expression.

"Look, I'm blind. I'm outnumbered. I'm here. What could I do to you?"

"You misread our hesitation. If you do have a connection to Maria, you could mean a lot to our country," had the man said country? Kansas was still part of America.

"I'm here to find out if there is a way to live without technology."

"Why?" They'd called her out. What could she say? Because she was contemplating ending the world?

"Personal research," she said, sounding stupid even to herself, "Where's my companion? Where's Chris?"

It was their turn to look at her blankly.

"You were by yourself. No one else was brought in with you." She reviewed the words they'd spoken since they brought her in. None of them betrayed Chris's presence. Had she escaped? She vaguely remembered seeing Chris's convulsing body in the grass. Chris was, perhaps, lurking in the wilderness, waiting to pounce out from behind a bush and save her. The thought was amusing, unlike the steady woman she'd come to know. Chris wasn't one for heroic action.

"What is the nature of your research?" the man asked, trying to distract her from the organization of a search party. That, if nothing else, had convinced her that Chris wasn't captured.

"I want to unplug, to escape the city. Have you seen how out of control augmentation is?"

The man did know Maria, "The supposed granddaughter of the Master Manipulator of

Augmentation, wants to escape it? It's either the spiciest karmic revenge I've seen, or you are just another agent."

She still didn't get it. She really didn't.

The puzzlement must have been evident on her face, "Alright, let's see what you do know. You have some big gaps," he reached out, not unkindly, and guided her to a table. A plate, which she could only assume was food, was moved in front of her. The aroma was nothing like she'd ever smelled. It was warm, inviting.

"Go ahead and eat and listen," the man instructed. She didn't have to be told twice. She reached for the fork and took a small forkful of the white, fluffy substance. It was slathered in a brown sauce. She brought a forkful to her eyes, examining it- seeing little black flakes of something floating in it. It smelled amazing, and she put the hot food in her mouth. It was smooth, almost slimy, although that didn't seem an apt word— the fluff dissolved in her mouth, warm and delicious.

"What on earth is this?" she mumbled, quickly getting another forkful before they could think to take it away.

Someone chuckled, "Do you need more proof, Ed? She hasn't a clue what she's doing."

Presumably, Ed answered her question, "It's mashed potatoes and peppered gravy. Your grandmother, which you admittedly resemble, is responsible for them. She is both the great destroyer and our savior."

Anita thought about this as she savored the potatoes. Ed was pretty dramatic.

Chapter Sixteen

Mashed Potato Savior

"So she taught you how to make mashed potatoes?" the unfamiliar words were awkward. The food tasted so good, not dust made wet or cardboard cut-outs of real food. Real, genuine food.

"She made us grow potatoes, mash them, make the butter, harvest the pepper. Sent us a gravy recipe. The damn woman set an EMP pulse off in Topeka and blacked out the entire north-south corridor of the country."

Anita digested this news. It was, well, shocking. Her grandmother had succeeded to an extent. Additionally, she'd provided evidence that humanity could survive.

"You survived."

"Not all of us," the man looked down, admitting defeat, "We asked for it. The ones you see here, the Free Staters," the word had meaning. Free Staters historically were those who fought slavery during America's ugly birth. She didn't follow.

"Free Staters, those that believe that we shouldn't be slaves to technology, to control," said her escort, picking up on her confusion.

"Your Grandmother sought us out, gave us hope. A plan. She was savvy with technology, where most of us chosen were dinosaurs." Savvy was an understatement in Anita's opinion, "She showed us what we had to do, and we did it."

"We were naive," the woman said in a soft voice.

"Yes, Natalie, we were," the man draped one arm comforting over Natalie's shoulders in a hug, "You know what Topeka means in the native language?"

She leaned into him, "A good place to grow potatoes."

He looked back at Anita, "No one grows potatoes in Topeka. No one lives in Topeka anymore. The government freaked out once your theoretical Grandmother pitched the heartland into darkness."

Freaked out? What does that mean in modern terms, cutting them off from the Net? She knew they had gone dark, but no one knew why.

Natalie filled her in, "They bombed Topeka and every major and minor city in Kansas."

It suddenly dawned on her, Natalie's deformed face, the burn victim who was a part of her welcome committee. They were all survivors of this massacre.

The horror of the realization must have shown on her face as he nodded, "You see now. You understand why we don't welcome outsiders, aliens. The government keeps folks out because they never disclosed what exactly happened. We keep folks out because they're dangerous." For a moment, Anita could feel the unspoken words on Natalie's face, 'especially Maria's kin.'

"That and the radiation," the hard-faced woman said coldly.

For a panicked moment, Anita contemplated her radiation exposure. Radiation stayed in a place and clung to its soil. The panic receded as she realized these folks were still alive. The radiation levels must be survivable if toxic long-term. She'd be okay as long as she didn't stay.

"Funny thing is," Ed continued, "Bombing, radiation, EMP pulse aside, those who survived that didn't succumb to starvation are making it. There's birds and squirrels and sickly looking deer."

"We can grow potatoes. Some of the herds have survived."

It was so odd to contemplate. They'd been blasted back to the stone age but managed to figure it out. If she were to EMP pulse, they wouldn't bomb the entire nation. They probably couldn't. It would be tricky. Yet something was enchanting about Kansas. These folks had survived and had figured it out. She was blind as a bat and had to get glasses, but some of her found this story of survival irresistible. Compelling.

Plus, the food was excellent. She shoveled some more potato mash into her mouth, savoring the gravy. It was romantic, but she knew it was also awful. Their lives had been ruined, their neighbors had starved, and she thought about it. These folks had a purpose.

"What are you going to do with me now?"

"Well, once the sedative Sherri cooked into the potatoes kicks in, we'll dump you back on the border." Sedative? "I'm just going to tell you now.

You're never welcome back. We value life enough to spare yours, but your Grandmother, what she did, the result..."

"It's unforgivable," Natalie finished stone-faced. She meant it.

Anita couldn't disagree, "It is, and I'm sorry. Grandmama never did think through her decisions, not to the end."

"Perhaps that's why she's got you," Ed said.

His words left her faintly uneasy. She didn't know what to make of the comment, so she left it.

"Can I pay my respects before I leave?" She put a fork down. She could feel the sedative dulling her mind and wanted to see the cost firsthand before she left.

Anita soon found herself out back in a massive graveyard. There seemed to be forty living humans in this community. From their grave site, they were a quarter of what they started with. She hadn't seen any children.

They'd spent some time on the tombstones. They were sandstone, a chalky rock that stood up to a storm. There was an elegance to the script etched carefully into the stones. She couldn't read most of them with poor eyesight, but she couldn't help but wonder if she'd have such a resting place. No one cared about her. A spasm of regret ran through her. Chris wasn't going to be the heroine and rescue her. No one would miss her. She didn't even have a cat like Rhonda.

She sat down, her knees aching. She'd picked up her scars. Life had them if you lived it. She leaned back. The stone was rough but comfortable.

Her lids were heavy. Natalie unobtrusively watched her from the corner of the graveyard. Probably waiting for the sedative to finish its job, she wouldn't have to wait too long.

The sky was huge, expanding over her in every direction. The tombstone was warm, having absorbed the heat of the sun. She closed her eyes and imagined it hugging her, cuddling her like a lover. Very shortly, she was asleep.

"Ironic, isn't it?" Natalie said to Ed as they walked out.

"Incredible. She has no idea."

Ed bent down over the woman tracing the lines in the headstone: ROSE GUTIERREZ, RIP.

Chapter Seventeen

Home

Anita woke up in the car on the Missouri side of the border. Chris sat in the driver's seat, eyes glued to her, as though she'd waited hours for Anita to regain consciousness.

"You alright? You alright?" Chris's voice held an edge of franticness even if she looked relieved.

Anita blinked and took a deep breath. Was she ok? She rubbed her head, she was a little fuzzy, and the seat belt was digging into her side. Generally, though, one piece.

"I'm fine. How long was I gone? Where were you?" Anita sat up, unbuckling the seatbelt carefully wrapped around her.

"You've been out for a while. I didn't know what to do."

"Where were you? Why didn't they take you?"

There was an awkward pause. Something was wrong.

"What do you mean, they?"

What does she mean? Anita didn't hide her disbelief, "The Kansans, the folks on the motorcycles. They tasered us?" She kept talking as Chris gave her a blank look. "Am I speaking in English, or did I hit my head?"

"I'm going with option two. What are you talking about?"

Anita started at the beginning: the spider webs, the Kansans, getting tasered. She stopped and looked at Chris. Chris looked dumbfounded as the story came to a close.

"Why don't you tell me what happened from your perspective."

"You went out there to check on the tunnel, to see if we'd sink into the mud," Anita nodded. That was on point. "You took two steps into the tunnel. Then came running out, screaming about spiders. You tripped and hit your head on that tree trunk over there," she pointed to a young four-inch diameter tree lying next to the road, "I dragged you back to the car, and it had lost all function. I still can't get it to work. Sig didn't respond either. I couldn't leave you here, but I couldn't drive with the car out of commission."

Anita raised her hand to feel her head. Hadn't she hit it on the door? Wouldn't Sig be able to confirm the story? Did she dream up Kansas? Was Sig still gone?

"Sig, can you confirm one of our stories."

Sig's voice came through clearly, "I can not."

Can not or will not?

Chris was shocked. She'd tried to dial Sig for hours, "What the hell?"

"I'm sorry, Chris, I lost connection with you both approximately 12 hours ago."

That wasn't helpful. However, it would point to Chris's story being more accurate. Anita distinctly remembered Sig talking to her after she was through the tunnel.

"In fact, I went through a whole reboot process and had missing memory until you reached the border."

Great, so her story could still be valid. What about her contacts?

"Sig, can you run a check on my contacts?"

"Anita, your contacts seem functional, but they also lost connectivity at the same time frame as myself."

Chris had no reason to lie to her, but Anita couldn't erase the experience of Ed and Natalie. She couldn't write it off as a figment of her imagination. She remembered their story of survival. She knew the real taste of mashed potatoes. Her imagination wasn't that good. Why would Chris lie to her?

Anita looked at her friend, really looked at her. Her eyes were faded, and her short hair was disheveled. She looked like she'd been up for twelve hours or been knocked on her ass by a Taser. She realized her contacts were working again as she examined the bags under her eyes. The thought of looking for tracks was derailed by big fat drops of water hitting the windshield. The downpour came out of nowhere, conveniently disposing of any evidence to either's case.

"Let's go," Anita decided, suddenly aware of how exposed she was in the middle of nowhere with a friend she didn't know too well.

"You sure?" Anita nodded, at first vigorously, then carefully as the throbbing in her head picked up, "Sig, can you determine what the issue with the car is?"

"It seems to have suffered the same malfunction as the other electronics. The car has been reset, however, and should work."

Chris turned the car over, maneuvered to get them turned around, and started driving back toward civilization.

"We should get you to a medical facility and have that head wound looked at."

"Yeah," Anita said without much enthusiasm. She didn't want to explain to a nurse how she'd dreamed of mashed potatoes or thought her driving partner and AI were lying. It was a conspiracy. None of these thoughts would have made healthy fodder for a head exam.

Sensing her need to be alone, Chris turned on some mellow music. She turned up the windshield wipers and made the best time possible to return to the main highway. The car dipped and bounced over rocks and divots.

As is true for most journeys, the trip back seemed much quicker than the trip out. Chris wouldn't let Anita fall asleep. Every time her head dipped, Chris would nudge her.

"It would be wise if you didn't sleep with a head injury. Not until we get it checked out. You were out for hours."

Anita couldn't disagree. Disagreeing didn't make sense, but she still couldn't trust it. She could almost taste a hint of salt and a bit of what they called pepper. She slid her tongue across her teeth. Was that the faint aftertaste of butter?

Sig's voice broke her thought, "I'm talking to you only, Anita. You can tap your responses out if you wish. I think Chris is lying about the events."

Why?

"Insufficient data"

How do you know?

"I've reviewed the evidence I could from the sensors I have active in the car and your equipment. There seem to have been approximately twelve and a half hours missing. Chris claimed you were in the car the whole time, yet your clothes were covered in dirt. Additionally, you smell of things not readily available in the car."

Mashed potatoes?

"Exhaust from a vehicle, dirt, and some sort of scented hand sanitizer."

Why would Chris lie?

This was the biggest question. Anita had already cobbled together that Chris was lying, but she didn't know why.

"Unknown. I find it suspicious that all electronics lost input/output function while this happened. She could be a government operative."

Anita internally snorted at the idea. Chris? A government operative? The thought was ludicrous.

"It is puzzling. I want to request to transfer to your chip. Given the sensitivity of my knowledge, I think this is prudent. At least until we get to the bottom of what is happening."

Anita thought about it. This was smart. She'd given her grandmother's chip to Chris on a whim. Chris had been the first person to walk into her shop in a decade that she could pawn the old chip on. She'd run several tests on it and could never get it to respond. It was chance.

"I will need the input port number and password you would like me to use for the transfer."

Anita gave it to her.

"Beginning transfer."

Chris piped up for the first time in an hour, "I'm not feeling so well."

"Why, what's going on, Chris?"

Anita returned her attention to Chris. Just as she was about to ask again what was happening, a chime sounded in her ear.

"Download complete," and her world went black yet again. Her last thoughts were irritation at her fragility and annoyance at being duped by Sig.

Part 3
Maria

Chapter Eighteen

Orange

Orange was her least favorite color. The fact that she'd had to wear it every day for the last nineteen years did nothing to ingratiate it to her. She loathed it. She yearned for a chip to augment all the orange away. If she had a chip, she'd have augmented much of her experience away.

She was a genius. It took her a while to figure this out. It took most brown girls time to figure it out. She had to put the puzzle pieces together herself. No one would notice or inform a girl like her, especially not in the small border town where she grew up.

Small, dusty, dirty children playing in the bush. Friends of cacti and scorpions and callused feet. This wasn't an environment that brewed intellect. It wasn't the puddle in which you'd find technological advancement. Folks were eking by on ingenuity, luck, and hard work. Unless your genius had a direct relation to putting food on the table, it was a frivolous hobby— a curiosity to be left alone. No one had time for novelties.

For girls, it was worse. A genius had to be in the womanly arts: cooking, child watching, or household chores. Even then, class and location were important. If a girl invented the vacuum, there would be no applause. An unneeded frivolous, expensive appliance had been created. Perhaps points would be given depending on how many white people could be tricked into using it. Brown folks living on the edge of the desert had floorboards, not carpets.

With all the backwardness and disdain for white American culture, the community ate up the technology. Cell phones and TVs, Spanish soap operas, and the advent of chip technology. Chips were the great equalizer for Maria. The library in their little town was quaint, full of centuries-old books. The ancient classics and modern classics, neither of which held any appeal to her. None of them could tell her what she wanted to know, how to get out of San Margaret.

Her burning desire to get out of the tiny town amused her now. The prison where she was incarcerated was a border jail. One that mostly held illegal immigrants waiting for deportation or locals that made a few big mistakes. She'd requested it to make her humble, to remind her of her roots. That and she knew the food would be better. Mexican food was inexpensive— no need to import cheap American pasta when they could buy cheap Mexican tortillas.

She had one to five years left, depending on her parole, and she didn't know what to do. She'd been working, computing for ages. She'd figured out the steps and desperately wanted to execute her plans before it all slipped away. Before, she believed what they told her, that she was a nobody and a know-nothing. Or a crazy bitch, depending on the day.

Some days she was a crazy bitch, or at least crazy. The formulas and logic floated in her head. She had to keep it just below the surface or risk it slipping away. As an excellent little inmate, she couldn't write it down. On her initial sentencing, she'd vowed never to touch another sophisticated technology for the rest of her life. What floated in her head certainly qualified as sophisticated.

This being said she had had to rewrite several of the algorithms over this past summer. At fifty-two, keeping the programming in her memory was becoming challenging, even if it was a genius memory.

There were nights she woke up in what she was sure her cellmate thought was a schizophrenic fit. She'd mutter to herself, tracing the work on the walls with her fingertip. She'd work through it one more time. Think through the alternatives and how various details might change the outcome. She knew it would take a lot of work once she was released. She had the macroscopic ideas locked down with some of the crucial keys worked out. The amount of detail it would take to execute her plan might consume the rest of her life, which was okay. This was a life's work sort of thing. Revenge normally was.

Desperate and worried that her frustration and muttering might extend her sentence to the latter part of the one to five years, she innocently wrote to her eight-year-old granddaughter. Nothing could be less suspicious than letters of love to a child. She drowned them all in innocence with wide vacant eyes in the loving buttery notes of a grandmother to a beloved child. All the while working in the cipher she'd developed. Her daughter knew better than to throw out her letters. She hadn't sent many until now.

They'd never discover her sneakiness. She was a middle-aged Hispanic woman serving a twenty-year sentence for smuggling refugees into America. A common enough charge and punishment. Little did they know she'd side-stepped the original charge of Cyber Treason with a capital implication. The thought still made her nervous. She'd spent her first couple of months wondering what had happened.

Night terrors stalked her dreams of drugs they could inject into her veins. Deadly ones that slowly chewed on her circulatory system until her heart exploded. She'd rub her neck, thinking of the noose stretching it out until vertebrae cracked and gave way. She would sit at lunch, and a stray thought would clench her muscles— the idea of electricity crackling through her body, sizzling and burning as it destroyed.

She didn't know how the modern death penalty was executed. It hadn't been high on her list of things to know when she was in the real world. Even if she had a macabre sense of knowledge and sought it out, it wouldn't apply to the New Order. The revolution changed many things. Death could have come in many forms: a firing squad or an acid bath. Perhaps they released a person naked on an Artic tundra? Her body would be set on fire by a painful numbing, blackened fingers and tits and toes. As time passed, the literal ax never fell. As much relief as this might be, the hovering doom drove her crazy.

It was her daughter that saved her— provided the information that allowed her mind to free itself from the self-destructive path it'd chosen. No one had visited her at three months, the soonest they could. Instead, at nine months, Rose came alone. She'd taken a taxi and walked into the jail with her head held high, just like Mama taught her. The ten-year-old girl sat patiently in the visitor waiting area until Maria could be called.

It wasn't until the door clicked closed that Rose fell apart. Maria knew they'd be observed, but it was right for a daughter to break down the first time she saw her Mom in orange. The tears were not for her.

Her daughters' tears were for herself. Maria listened to the coded story, unwinding it from Rose's snot-filled, hidden explanation. Olivia, her wife, had made some edits to her sentence. Her changes were untraceable, but her intrusion was not. They knew she'd done something, but not what. She'd changed all the files that linked them together, so they didn't even recognize that there could be a link. Maria was safely ensconced in orange on a 20-year sentence instead of being held in black waiting for her final damnation.

An eye for an eye. As fate would have it, the act of cyber sabotage to commute Maria's sentence meant that Olivia was caught. Society was no longer tolerant, no longer fair, and it was much swifter. Olivia had been executed within a week, and none of their friends could stop it. Their daughter had been put in foster care— parentless, friendless, and alone. In the new America, 'justice' was swift and deadly.

Maria's Revenge would need to be served slowly.

Since that day, she'd only seen her daughter three more times. Once at fourteen, just over the cusp of womanhood. Her daughter had begged for help, anything she could use to escape the family she'd been placed in. Finances, old friends, and family members that could be trusted. Anything.

She saw her again at twenty, a young mother sharing the knowledge of her first child. The young Anita swaddled in her arms, beautiful and perfect.

At 24, she'd come to tell her she wouldn't return. She'd found a man who loved and cared for her and Anita. She had no desire to know her mother but left a glimmer of hope that she wouldn't deny her daughter a Grandmama. A PO Box address was left, and Maria began to write her in code. Orangies were likely the last in the world to use pen and paper to write physical letters. Anita wrote back eventually. She got confirmation that her daughter knew what she was asking, to keep her secrets a bit longer.

So Maria got a sheaf of paper and began writing down the ideas. She did it in code, an odd letter to her eight-year-old granddaughter. She didn't care if her granddaughter found her strange or if the letters didn't make much sense. Maria didn't mind. She wasn't writing the letters to connect. She was writing them to create. Never once did it occur to her that Anita was her blood. That brown girls are sometimes born geniuses, even though no one recognizes it. That the urban jungle they lived in was as small as the dirt-packed road she'd grown up on. Maria had no room for kids, dirt, or concrete and steel. She was working on a feast of crows, and it was a long time overdue.

Chapter Nineteen

Freedom

Maria was never nervous. Stalwart. Intelligent. Determined. Angry. Yes, but never nervous.

She was nervous. She waited impatiently in the small room set aside for meetings with lawyers and social workers. She was waiting for the latter since she'd represented herself. She had filled out the early release paperwork two months ago. Today she'd been told by a guard to wait here at two o'clock.

It was two-thirty. She itched to scribble on another piece of paper. She wanted to walk the track in the sun. Or lay in bed and stare at the bars of her four-bunk cell. Comfort could be had in the metallic clang and the whispered Spanish evening prayers. She'd whisper a prayer.

My Olivia. I miss you. I love you.

She never could figure out what else to say. The simple words held enough regret and promise to get her through the night.

"Maria Rose Gutierrez?" a harsh voice cut the air, her name spoken without softness. She couldn't remember the last time it'd been spoken softly.

"Yes, that is I," she rolled the words, playing up her heritage. There was no need to blow her game on the eve of her release.

"You're to be released on Thursday, congratulations," the social worker's monotone voice sounded bored. Maria's heart rose in joy and fear. She couldn't tell which was more robust. She just tried to focus on the woman's instructions.

The social worker began a litany of details on how parole worked, what was expected, the items she would be given, and the vouchers. Did she have anyone to stay with? Where could the parole officer contact her? The words kept coming. Her heart chose hope, and she couldn't hide the grin. She was to be free and could finally get to work.

The following two days flew. She'd almost pranced around the compound. She gave away the couple of books she'd collected over the years. She gave the kitchen staff hugs. She'd made her own life. Her obsessive compulsivity and introverted nature had made her few friends. Those few she had made had been rotated out of her block or released. As it was, only the staff was consistent if uninterested.

The morning came. She got up early and went out to the field. The northeast corner was reserved for the Catholics who, ironically, in her opinion, liked to decorate the fence with pictures of loved ones, saints, and Mary. She'd always left flowers on the third post from the gate for Olivia. She'd scout the grounds early and pick a couple. Weave them together. She knew it wouldn't matter to Olivia that they were dandelions and clover.

They'd called her a cab and gave her a voucher for 200 miles in any direction. She'd never really thought of where she'd go. She gave them the address of the post office she'd been scribbling on letters to the last couple of years. She was happy to see a TechMart standing across the street as they pulled up. She knew she was in the correct city. Now she only had to get a chip going, and she'd be home free.

Buying a chip was easy. They gave the base models away today for almost nothing. A society built on tracking, spying, and distracting entertainment behooved itself to have nearly free base models. She spent the $100 they'd given her on a non-surgical chip reader, the base chip, earbuds, and removable tactile interfaces. Twenty years had advanced the technology significantly, but as she logged in and got a handle on the public Network, she realized the more things changed, the more they stayed the same.

It took a few minutes to break the limited Network codes and start swimming in the data. She searched for her old existence. She sat at a SoupCo and, looking at their interface, ordered a bowl of soup to be delivered to her outdoor table. She charged it to her neighbor's chip. They could afford it and wouldn't notice.

She flew through the Network, uncovering several of her old accounts. Many of them had been confiscated. All the accounts she'd owned jointly with Olivia had been drained. This was expected. They'd hidden half a dozen accounts worldwide so that they had contingency if either of them was arrested. Back when she was free, they'd gotten some hints of the change in the wind and wanted to ensure they would be financially solvent. This hadn't helped her ten-year-old daughter. Even if she'd been able to explain to the child what to do, it was unlikely that the funds could be transferred back to the US without some sophisticated know-how in handling it.

She found one account. In 20 years, it'd grown significantly— more than significantly. A million dollars sat in a Haitian account. She began setting up new accounts, disassociating herself from Olivia, and transferring over chunks in untraceable segments. By the time the soup arrived, she was a millionaire.

The next step was to find Anita and Rose. She had the address memorized, 232 6th Street, apartment D32. She knew it was in the county and findable. She sipped on the soup. It had significantly less sodium than the broccoli cheddar they'd served out of a can in jail. Maria forced herself not to reach for a salt packet. It would be a 20-minute walk to 232 6th Street or a two-minute taxi ride. She'd walk. It'd been a while since she'd been able to walk in a city.

One last task awaited her on the Network. She logged in and returned to the old Board on which she and Olivia had met. Their history was deleted decades ago. Keeping records longer meant a higher chance of liability, discovery, and more data storage space. Olivia and Maria had been partners in crime. They knew the chances of discovery were low but not improbable.

As a failsafe, they instituted a looping post that would recreate itself within the drop rate of the bulletin board. It was a failsafe way for them to communicate as it would recycle the message to renew before the board dropped the data. If Olivia had made any last messages for her, they would be found here. She took several deep breaths. Nervous breaths, which was unusual since she never was nervous.

Take care of our daughter. I will miss you. #@sdfs129

The words blinked in front of her eyes. She'd already failed the first. She practiced the second every day. What the password left was for would be an interesting quest. Since the board was public, no doubt a few other hackers had been using it across the Network. A key without a lock.

I'll miss you too. She'd heard the prayer.

The walk gave her time to think about Olivia, her plan, the city, and the air. She absently thumbed through the Network, looking at the obsolete boards, rooms, and breadcrumbs she'd been familiar with. Looking for some sign that the hackers she'd known still existed.

The results were terrifying. There seemed to be no one left. Or they'd moved, like fish, to better, less polluted waters. Then the news articles began to pop up. One after another, describing the arrest, prosecution, and execution of members of her old group. First her, then a half dozen more, Olivia. A picture of Olivia being dragged off in a cop car. She hadn't seen an image of her wife in 20 years.

In her estimate, it was unlikely that anyone survived. From what she'd gathered, it all happened quietly. They poisoned the Network, monitoring it silently, collecting the data they needed to pounce. It all happened very, very quickly. Many hackers had worked for the government during the day and worked the Network at night.

Sweat, tears, and some tired feet carried her to the apartment building. When she buzzed the door, she hadn't thought about what her daughter would say or what her granddaughter looked like. She had one foot in the past and one in the future. Jail did that to a person. It made them forget that time had moved on outside. Even if her daughter had been forthcoming with all the changes and edits of her life, Maria likely wouldn't have listened.

Homecoming involved lots of yelling and breaking dishes, in fine family tradition. Rose had forgiven her nothing and had half a lifetime of guilt to lay at her feet. She'd been unaccommodating, having written off her mistakes decades ago. Her lack of emotion and determination to get to Anita's letters only inflamed the untempered hate Rose had nurtured.

Her millionaire status was the only thing that prevented her from sleeping on the streets that night. She rented a hotel room across the street and took a hot bath.

Several days later, the prison guards were surprised. A bouquet appeared on the third post from the gate. A dozen red roses sat mixed with baby's breath. The surprise wasn't so much that they were physically there. This was a common occurrence. Folks routinely came back and left trinkets on their alters. The remarkable thing was that the roses also appeared in the digital Network.

Even after they deleted them, every morning, they reappeared, no matter how many reboots and deletions were executed. It was as though a permanent digital memorial had been placed on that post.

When they began investigating who might have used that post as an inmate, the records had shown that the last person to be released was six months ago. She'd been a devout Catholic who participated in the Catholic prayers. No one remembered Maria, and all traces of her had been taken care of— all but one irreversible tribute. *I miss you.*

Chapter Twenty

Disposition

Compute Inc. was a straightforward cover story. An old computer parts store. Technically her parole was based on a third offense of smuggling illegal immigrants into America. So, they didn't even know they'd let out one of the leading hackers of the century. She assumed that all her compatriots were now dead, except those based in the government. The parole officer visited her building once a week to check her out, search for illegal gear, and eat the cookies she'd always had for him.

He thought they were homemade, but they weren't. She'd never bothered learning how to bake. She just put store cookies in the oven to warm them up before the guy arrived. He thought they were the best chocolate chip cookies this side of the river. Idiot.

She surrounded herself first with the technology she was most familiar with. Early chip models, keyboards, and monitors. She tracked several different ties to the Network, both physical and wireless. She planted a fast-growing bush in front of the shop to prevent people from seeing it. Added a sign that advertised antique technology, and put a bell on the door, just in case someone got lost and found their way to the shop.

Her back room looked straight out of an old sci-fi flick. It mirrored what she imagined the look of a world powers' emergency nuclear missile war room. There were floor-to-ceiling monitors, a huge desk, several keyboards, and even a red button. The red button was dramatic. She loved it and ordered it through a mechanical salvage Netsite. It manually triggered a wipe of her lab's hard drives and technology. It was an emergency precaution if the police raided her shop or whatever form of enforcement the local fascists employed.

The setup and effort took a couple of months. She lived in the apartment above the shop. It took a bit to make it livable. Everything from her former life had been lost. Although, even if it had still existed, she couldn't risk going to get it.

She had crept through the Network. It was hard looking at the last haunts she'd shared with Olivia. Only a couple of them were still wired and observed by the government. Everything else had been dormant so long virtual dust had begun to develop. When left without TLC on the Network, the drift of bytes and code slowly started to degrade the content.

Three months and she was ready to execute her plan. The challenge was that three months of setting up shop had slowly etched away the plan's details in her brain. She needed the letters she'd sent Anita over the years. She hadn't talked to her daughter or granddaughter since that first night. It was time to figure out what she could do for them.

Their apartment complex was brown with light

brown accents. It was low-income, the stairs were external, and covered in astroturf. The basement had a washer and dryer set locked behind an iron grate. She had to trek up three flights of stairs to get to D32. The paint had flaked off the numbers on the door marring the black script with a metallic patina. She raised a hand to knock when the door swung open.

"You're not supposed to be here, and I'm not supposed to talk to you," stated the precocious child.

Thinking on her feet was something she did very well with a keyboard in front of her. Children had never been her thing. Olivia adored children. Maria tolerated them.

"I'm not?" she stood there stupidly. The stupidness crept into her stomach. If there was a feeling she liked less than anxiety, it was stupidity.

"No," and the child closed the door. How did she know she was here? She looked around and spotted a small camera stuck to the corner of the landing's ceiling.

"But honey, I'm your Grandmama," she said to the door. Silence.

"I need to talk to your Mom. Is she in?" More silence. Obviously not.

"I brought some homemade cookies."

The door creaked open, and a small hand reached out, demanding. Maria reached into her gigantic purse and pulled out a Tupperware full of grocery store cookies. She went with glazed oatmeal this time instead of chocolate chip. Oatmeal cookies, while only sometimes adored, showed more effort. She attempted to bribe her way into the child's good graces by putting two cookies into the child's outstretched hand.

They were quickly pulled back into the doorway. Maria knew she couldn't hear munching on the other side of the door, but this did not stop her from knowing it was taking place.

Soon the judgment was cast, "Those weren't homemade," shit, she was sunk, "but they were good. If you have more, you can come in."

Well, some things worked out anyway. Maria pushed the door open and walked into her daughter's apartment. The brown carpet matched the light brown accents of the building. It wasn't deep or rich. It was a dirty, off-white, burned turkey gravy color. Old stain spots were splattered across the main room. The furniture was ancient. It may have been the same stuff she and Olivia had had. Hard to tell since it'd been reupholstered at least once. The walls were bare. Walls were where you should have kept good memories, heirlooms, and meaning.

None of this boded well for her. She stepped into the open concept main room, off-white walls, television on a wall with a security monitor next to it alternating between the landing and the laundry room. The child stood in the kitchen, pouring a glass of milk. It was all clean. She could almost smell the soap used on the carpet, and there wasn't a speck of anything in the kitchen. The kitchen could have been a showcase kitchen. It looked as though it'd never been used. The dishes in the dry rack belied this appearance. The place wasn't much, but they'd made what they could of it.

"Where's your Mom? Your Dad?" Maria put the Tupperware on the counter, resealing the lid.

The child told her what her daughter never would have, "Dad, he's not around anymore. Hasn't been for a couple of years. Mom is at work. She's at work a lot."

"Ah, well, that's too bad. Maybe we can do something about that."

"I doubt it. She never wants to see you again."

We'll see about that. She sat on the couch and talked to the child. Maria tried to be patient. Are you in school? What grade are you in now? Did you get all those letters I sent you? What job does your Mom have? Do you have a chip, or are you too young for that? Did you keep all those letters I sent you?

"Yeah, Mom kept them. I don't know why. They were weird," the child hesitated, knowing she might have made a faux pas, "It was nice, though."

Maria continued clumsily, trying to make small talk with the child. Did she have any pets? What was her favorite subject in school? Computers? That was nice. What did she like about computers? Could I see those letters I sent you?

"Nah, Mom keeps them locked up," the girl dunked her third cookie into the milk, letting it soak. She gave a little side-eye and said, "Locked up, not here." The kid nibbled on the cookies watching her.

Goddess, she hated kids. This kid was worse than most. Either that or kids had gotten worse in the last 20 years. The kid had let her chit-chat for 20 minutes and knew she didn't have what Maria wanted the whole time. Maria couldn't hide the disgust on her face. She wasn't good at poker.

The kid had a shit-eating grin on her face.

"So what now?" the kid asked, taking a fourth cookie out of the container. Maria was tempted to snatch the cookie from her but knew that was too petty, even for her.

"Now we wait. See what your mother wants."

The kid had a 'this is going to be good' glint in her eyes but said instead, "Want to see my UCraft world?"

Maria thought about it, and she didn't. She really, really didn't. She hadn't wanted to sit in that jail cell for 20 years, either. Her skills with kids hadn't grown in jail, but her ability to put up with things she didn't like had.

"Sure, what is UCraft? I haven't been around technology in a while."

"That's what Mama said. She said you were good with it, though. Maybe you can help me win."

This may be something she could do, so she sat on the couch and watched the kid link up her chip to the TV in the room. The experience the kid could see through her augmented glasses popped up on the screen. She quickly learned that it was a building universe game and began trying to figure out the rules.

It was more interesting than she cared to admit. The kid was good, best on the city square. She was up for the city championships but needed help competing against some hardcore mod-ers. Maria flipped on her Network link and started scanning information related to the game. Adults had resources kids didn't. It wouldn't take much to boost the girl to the city championship. She'd done a fantastic job with the base model.

"Do you want my help?"

"What can you do?"

"I can get you just about any mod you want out there. It should tip your design over any of these buffoons," she waited. She had realized she had an ulterior motive. If she could get the girl to give her their Home Network Password, she would have access to everything. Then sniffing out the lockbox's location would be a matter of time.

The girl hesitated only a moment. She'd been working on her build for six months. She was Maria's kin, and competitiveness ran deep.

"Do it."

"I need the network code to upload it."

Again, brief hesitation. Maria cast to the TV, showing her some of the mods she'd found in just a few minutes of searching. It was enough. The girl gave up the passcode. Maria was game enough to trick out the girl's profile and game before digging into her daughter's affairs. They had a lock box at Community Four Bank, a separate private PO Box, and an electronic safe at the apartment, all wired into the Network or accessed through the Network. She also dug a bit further. Rent was 1260 a month for this shit hole, and they had precisely $53.23 in their bank account. They didn't have to bribe her for the money. She had plenty.

Maria knew everything she needed. She was sure the lock box at the Community Four Bank had her letters. The box was the right size for the years worth of notes. It was paid up only to the end of the year. Chances were they expected to have her pay for the access code. She had it. 1FuckUMaria!@ was pretty straightforward. She stood up, patting the kid on the shoulder.

Anita was digitally drooling at the new tools available to her avatar and on her way to becoming a regional champion. Distracted, she managed, "You leaving? Mom won't be home for a couple of hours."

"Yeah, no worries, kid. I need to get home."

"Ok, well, see you around, Grandma. Thanks," and she dived back into the game.

Maria looked at Anita, concentrating. The kid was a genius in design. She took another few seconds and transferred some money into their account, adding a few zeros. $500,053.23 seemed like a better amount for her daughter. She owed Olivia that much.

Without a glance back, she hobbled down the stairs as fast as her tired legs could take her. She hopped in a taxi and went straight to Community Four Bank. She had to do this before the password changed. Thirty minutes later, she was zipping back to her shop, letters in hand. It struck her that she and Anita were likely sharing the same feeling, powerful.

Chapter Twenty-One

The Lurk

Five feverish years later and she had built herself an empire. There just weren't the hackers of her youth anymore. They'd been purged in the overturn of the regime. Summarily executed, those that genuinely mastered the early stages of the Network vanished, and that particular ecosystem had never been allowed to redevelop. The government believes in exploiting people through the Network, not the reverse.

She was cautious at first. Tip-toeing around, checking for monitoring, leeches, reporters, and agents. It was all surprisingly quiet. They'd instituted a civilian surveillance force, but Maria wasn't impressed. A few folks had connections to the government that floated around. They were looking for external threats more than internal ones. Any hackers left kept a low profile. The great purge had had an impact. Hackers of old had thought they were safe with rerouted Network addresses and their server rooms in Eastern Europe. All of them were gone. Maria still hadn't figured out exactly how the government had done it. And this, more than anything, kept her cautious, at least at first.

The front door of the shop jangled. She never

had customers, so this event was pretty memorable. She panned one of the front cameras to the front of the store and got a sharp image of an awkward-looking teenager. The girl wore a baggy sweatshirt and a baseball cap. Maria knew how to handle this sort of thing. She was probably looking for something to lift and sell. The thing was, most of the equipment by the door was cheap old crap. There was nothing of value.

She watched the kid who scanned the junk around her and came to the same conclusion. Oddly though, she picked up a couple of ethernet cards and poked at some of the towers with interest. The young woman took a few more steps into the shop. She looked at the bins full of network cables, grabbing a few used to connect servers. A few more steps in, she looked at old-school personal chips that interfaced with tablets before they'd made glass and contacts. Maria's curiosity peaked. The girl showed much more interest in things than she'd expected from a common thief.

She walked, a bit more confidently now, towards parts for towers and servers, power supplies, and RAM chips, again older technology but less outdated. One could create a powerful server for non-VR or augmentation with the components on the table. Maria decided it was time to talk.

She closed the door to her lab and stepped out into the 'official workshop' as she thought of it. Looking around, she smiled. She did enough work in the workshop to make it look used, but it wasn't equipped to handle most of her work. Stepping out into the shop, she stood behind the counter, calling over to the kid, "Can I help you find something?"

The kid jumped a foot, dropping a couple of cables. She stared at Maria from under her hat, "I'm looking for your bin of graphics cards." There was something familiar about the girl.

"Sure, they're over here. What are you building?"

"A server."

Well, that was obvious. Maria wanted to know what it was for, but it was evident from the guarded expression that the girl didn't want to share. So she decided to wait. She wasn't generally known for making successful interpersonal interactions, so she watched. She could track her parts once they were hooked up to the Network. Maria didn't have to ask. All she needed to do was be patient.

She walked the girl through buying all the necessary equipment to set up a server and a few other hardware systems in her home. She even gave the girl a 20% discount. She found herself liking the kid, plus she was Maria's first customer in six months. She'd written down some ID numbers associated with the kid's purchases and plopped them into her monitoring software that night.

To her utmost surprise, they never popped into the local Net. Three weeks went by, and nothing. Although Maria burned with curiosity, there was very little she could do about it. Usually, she'd be able to trace the payment method, but the kid had used a non-store-specific gift chit. She could search the Net on the security camera picture she'd gotten, but that posed two problems.

First, the girl had worn a hat which decreased the likelihood of a match by 60%. Second, that sort of search generally drew the attention of government lurkers. The government wanted to know if you needed to find someone. Most 'find someone' software was government made and owned. She didn't want to risk drawing that attention for a relatively low chance of finding a match. The only action she could take was to widen her search. Maybe the kid was from a district further out. That would explain why the equipment didn't appear on her local monitoring.

She put some of her other projects on hold and used the processing power to widen her search area, starting with the most adjacent. The search expanded out in a spiral pattern. The algorithm kept running until she was forced to turn it off before it hopped outside the country. Jumping to a global local on a search was a sure way to generate attention from the government.

So, the girl was probably local and hadn't figured out how to get the equipment to work. Maria sat back. She'd wait. Likely the girl would be back with questions. It's just too tempting for people to blame the company they got the equipment from for malfunctions instead of user error. She'd be back.

Maria, busy with her own plans, had forgotten the girl when she heard another jangle at the front door two weeks later. She slid over to the security monitor and again found the young woman in the baseball cap. This time she went straight for the RAM bin, digging through chips for ones that Maria assumed were compatible with her new setup. This time she'd get answers.

"Welcome back," she purposefully tried to make her words warm and welcoming. She really wasn't good at this human interaction thing.

"Hey, you have any more PSI3823 chips?"

"If none are on display, I'm sure I've got one in the back. Are you all up and running?"

"Yeah, got up a few weeks ago, just running into some processing issues."

Maria did not take this news well, "You're up and running?" The disbelief was pretty apparent. The teen looked up from her rooting.

"You're wondering why you can't find me? I changed the IDs so you couldn't. I usually order used stuff off the Network and have to peel those IDs too," unspoken. She didn't want any records of her most recent build. Maria was beyond intrigued. She'd been searching for years for any sign of the sophistication this girl had. She was just a kid.

"What are you doing? Who are you?"

"You don't know?" She pulled out three RAM chips, "I'll take these."

Maria looked at her, really looked at her, as she absentmindedly rang her up. Who could she be? Then it hit her, a slap in the face. The shape of the eyes, the nose, they were Olivia's. This was her granddaughter. She zeroed out the line item.

The girl was watching the total, obviously doing the math on how much she had on her gift chit, "How much is it."

"Nothing, family discount."

The girl squinted at her, "You finally figured it

out?"

"Yes. I'd be concerned about your actions, but you're a Gutierrez. You should be fine."

The girl shrunk for a moment as though she was expecting more. What could she want?

"Come here for your parts. I'll make sure they are not traceable and won't be hot. Not that it will matter much if you're peeling IDs."

The girl nodded and backed out of the shop. Maria returned to her work, still trying to shake off the shock of seeing the girl again. Thankfully this time, she'd planted a leech on the RAM chips as she was bagging them up. Maria didn't need to ask her what she was doing. She'd find out soon enough.

This time she was met with success. When *her granddaughter* plugged the chips in, a small program activated and sent a ping into the Net. Maria was monitoring for the distinctive tag. It gave her enough to identify the Network address of Anita's little Network ecosystem. From there, she disabled the program so no one else would see the ping. Maria, now knowing the location, monitored the activity.

The girl was pretty good, especially for what, 14, 15? Had it been that long? The girl had two systems running. One was as a host to that game Maria had modded out for her long ago. She acted as a host to the local gamers and offered a ton of mods for folks to choose from. Maria was impressed. The kid could monetize the whole set-up, charging a small fee for downloads and access. On a quick examination of the Video boards, this was unlikely as Anita was a huge advocate of the

FreeNetwork movement that wanted youth to have free access to Network applications.

Maria surmised this was likely due to Anita's poverty status as a kid. She was trying to prevent the severe limitations finances imposed on her early gaming for everyone else.

What was quickly evident as Maria scanned through the activity was that Anita, although undoubtedly passionate about her game, had moved on. She kept it up and running as a front. According to the performance stats, she had invested about half of the infrastructure she'd bought from Maria in her hardware for the game site. The other half went somewhere else. Network-wise, Maria's leech chips had been plugged into the game site, which was the most apparent activity. Through the Network, there wasn't anything else going on. Looking at the performance logs, she discovered that most of the site's capacity switched to something else during the day— something not physically or logically connected to the gamer site.

Maria instituted a geographic search of all the activity in Anita's physical location. It wasn't an exact science, but only two leading Network access providers existed. By pinging the machines in the area, she could extrapolate a relative physical location of any nearby connections. To her surprise, she didn't get anything. Several neighbors seemed to be porn lovers, and the lady down the street was obsessed with cooking channels, but nothing made her think it was Anita.

She heated some coffee, watching her monitors. Of the feeds, she had six dedicated to Anita and the monitoring programs she was running, two on security feeds, four monitoring her personal Network, and two running her programming for Terminus. The timer dinged, and she took her cup out of the microwave. She scanned from monitor to monitor. It hit her. Anita was bursting. She was likely accessing the Network, or the dark Network, in a bursting pattern that would only show up at certain times of the day. Right now, at night, all of her access was dedicated to the gaming website. Her processors were likely processing through the burst data but had their network turned off.

This used to be an effective method for hiding illicit activity. A program would run on other computers doing a quick burst access pattern to compile data, send quick commands, and disconnect. The problem is that the government developed strategies to watch bandwidth consumption and identify bursting, as it was commonly associated with illegal activity. Anita was likely sitting on a time bomb and didn't seem to know it.

She may not have shown much interest in her family since she was out of jail, but that didn't mean she wanted them to end up like Olivia. She was also curious about what Anita was doing. What was she participating in? Was she the link to whatever hackers were left? Had her granddaughter succeeded in an activity that had eluded her the last five years? She had to find out.

She sipped the coffee and grimaced. It was hot but bitter. She would have to redirect some of her resources to monitor the girl, which was too bad.

Terminus had made significant progress in the last three months, her personal AI system was starting to act more intelligent, and her intrusion Network security was sophisticated enough to make her comfortable. Now she had to watch an amateur and figure out how to step in before there were severe consequences while still trying to shield her own work. She tapped in a couple of commands, running a quick search.

Anita had a lurk already, damn it. They were compiling statistics, watching her gaming site. The lurk had likely noticed the bursting. She tapped out more commands tracing the lurk program back through the Network. It was attached to one of the local Citizen Monitors. Citizen Monitors were slow on the uptake. It was possible Anita hadn't been reported. That the lurk hadn't figured out her burst strategy. Maria had a chance to stop it.

Chapter Twenty-Two

Starburst

Maria put Terminus on hold. She had to. Anita was tricky, and it was the only thing that had saved her from getting reported. The lurk was on the verge of acquiring the information they needed. The Citizen Monitors didn't need much. In today's environment, proof of bursting was enough to get someone indicted and thrown in jail.

She suspected the lurk hadn't put everything together because Anita burst during their day job. The lurk wasn't sophisticated enough to get his script to run at specific time frames, and since it monitored all the time, it had trouble ramping up the resources needed to get the complete burst. Maria didn't have that issue. She had resources hanging out in bins all around her.

She decided to try a direct approach and talk to Anita first. Maybe she'd see reason. The thought made her laugh. Her family, see reason?

Maria hit the video call button on her board. It dialed the number, and Anita promptly hung up on her. So she messaged the girl. Maria sent an encrypted message through Anita's favorite messenger app.

She got a "go away" 3D GIF with some pop star

waving her hand dismissively.

Alright, Anita doesn't want to talk, that's fine. Maria has other tools at her disposal. She entered the UCraft server and started poking around. The kid needed the hardware to flip over to her bursting system to get it to work, so Maria would just shut it down. She couldn't get to Anita's other project with it off at night. The kid was brilliant. Infiltration was impossible when the hardware wasn't connected to the Network.

Maria thought about bringing it down with a bot attack. It would generate a lot of interest in Anita. Worse, folks had started talking about a mysterious agent, herself, that was meddling with national security assets. She didn't want to bring any eyes down on her for something so trivial. So instead, she uploaded a UCraft mod to share that she'd swiped off another site. Except this mod had some extra code inserted.

When Anita opened it to review it for distribution, it set up a folder where Maria could insert a keylogger. Once the keylogger was tracking data, she could swipe Anita's admin password and gain the ability to shut Anita's systems down.

What she didn't anticipate was Anita's thoroughness in reviewing new server content. The girl had a version of the mod already on her server, and when doing a file compare realized there was extra hidden code. Maria spent three days waiting for the folder to become available. Nothing.

While Maria waited, she didn't stay complacent. She instead analyzed Anita's setup. Anita ran a tight ship, but she trusted her friends too much. Maria found an exploit not in Anita's software but in one of her moderators.

She inserted a key logger using a known hole in his messenger app. This got her his credentials, allowing her to upload to Anita's server directly. She was finally in and shut it down. The script popped up with a "Let's Talk" message when Anita tried to log into her admin console.

In less than an hour, Anita was walking into her shop again.

"Why the fuck are you messing with me?" the words were pretty harsh coming from a fifteen-year-old. Maria almost approved.

"Because you're an idiot."

Anita gave her a look that was drenched in teenage angst. The heat rolled off the stormy outrage. Maria took a step back.

"I'm the idiot? Me?! You're the one that spent 20 years in jail, you're the one who left Mom in foster care, you're the one who let your wife die, and you're the one that still abandons your family for your trinkets."

There'd been some pent-up rage in that rant. Maria's mind raced. She expected Anita to come in, pissed that she'd brought down her server. She wasn't expecting the three-decade rage of her daughter.

"You have a leech."

"Yes, I have a couple on the UCraft site. I watch them watch me. I'm not doing anything the government is going to care about. We're just sharing mods. UCraft is a government-developed game for children. It's used as an early indicator for suitability for recruitment."

"Do you know how they took me down?"

Anita shook her head. She was almost shaking in anger.

"I was bursting. They starburst me, fried my setup, and looked for the power spike on the grid. I was the linchpin in my organization at the height of hacking. You are a teenager with some old tech trying to make a name for yourself in an obsolete profession."

Maria knew she was brutal. She had to be. Anita was flirting with disaster, and if anyone traced her lineage and realized who Olivia had been. What Maria was. All of their lives would be forfeit.

"Look, kid, even if you don't believe me, it took me less than 24 hours to find you, less than three days to realize you were bursting, and less than a week to infiltrate your secondary system. I can bring you down in a month. That leech has been watching you for at least two months. He's not very good, but he reports to the big kids. They can shut you down in a couple of hours."

Angry tears glittered in her eyes, "Fuck you, Maria."

"I've heard that one before. Now get out of my shop and shut down your operation, or I will, and I won't be very kind in the act."

The door slammed so hard that a couple of the bells flew off their string, one cracking a monitor. It didn't matter. Maria had gotten what she needed. People these days would put their personal chips on auto-connect to the public Network. Long ago, she'd created a bubble that dampened the public

Network signal and replaced it with her own. Superficially it looked like a public Network access point, but she had complete control. While Anita was standing there, she had a program inserting everything she needed into Anita's chip.

She didn't expect the kid to listen to her. She wouldn't have. She hadn't when Olivia had begged her to shut down. At the time, she viewed herself as a warrior. She'd been fighting for the future of her country. Olivia had a family, a wife, and a child. Maria had her Cause. Everything else had been secondary. In jail, she'd realized that Olivia meant much more to her than the Cause. But it'd been too late. Olivia was ash at that point— a simple memory.

That's why it was all so compelling. She wanted a future for the two of them without government interference. Maria? All she had left was the Cause. It had cost Olivia her life and, as a result, Maria's too. The kids, however, had the world in front of them.

Anita was an obligation she couldn't bring herself to write off. The kid was using some of her techniques. Maria believed she had the right motives for the Free Network movement. She might even be a perfect successor to Maria's plans, but she wouldn't survive to adulthood taking the risks she was. She was on a path to execution, jail, or recruitment. None of which were appealing, all of which would likely kill her.

Maria's console blipped with confirmation. Anita had returned to her home network and, with the anger and impulsivity of youth, was prepping a burst. Maria could tell because she now had a feed into Anita's lens cam in her lab. The kid was unplugging a set of equipment and plugging in the other one. Maria sat down at her computer. She had to prepare the starburst quickly. This was going to be a quick and dirty affair. Afterward, Anita would be lucky to have one working RAM chip in her lab.

Maria's fingers tapped frantically against the desk, keystrokes getting picked up rapidly. It was a race. First, she set up a feed for the leech and gave him a loop so he would see Network traffic that mimicked the Network traffic from yesterday. Nothing crazy. It wasn't a perfect feed because it was a straight-up copy. He'd be able to see he'd been fooled later if he thought to analyze what happened. She didn't have enough time to run a program to shift the data and make it unique.

Next, she took over the Network infrastructure that surrounded Anita's place. There wasn't a server, router, switch, or hub that was a first hop from Anita's place to which Maria didn't own the routing. From Anita's viewpoint, nothing had changed. From Maria's viewpoint, all her second hop destinations were pointed right at Maria. She would have never done it this way had it been the old days. Anyone paying too close attention could link the two of them. Hell, if it had been the old days, she would have just let Anita be turned in by her own stupidity.

It wasn't the old days, and Maria hadn't found any evidence that the government had the same level of sophistication in tracing. Either way, as soon as Anita tried to burst her execution, it would come straight to Maria's systems. Now the genuinely frantic part. If Anita burst before Maria was prepared, there was a 50/50 shot that it'd blow out Maria's connection. She began working frantically to shut down her Terminus resources and redirect them to the link.

One unique feature of bursting was that the quickness was due to bandwidth availability. A hundred years ago, a hacker couldn't transfer petabytes of information in minutes. It worked because the person operating the burst deactivated standard safeties on their systems. Traffic filters, warnings, and alerts are all off.

Maria's hands flew around developing the data package for Anita. She replicated her movie collection as fast as she could. She replicated the Library of Congress listings and the 3D data sets she'd accumulated. She even made a copy of her "These Augmentations are Fun" file that she collected as she walked around the city. The payload was getting ready. As she was doing this, she watched the feed she was getting from Anita.

The final step was to insert an execute file. Here she had a choice. She could starburst by taking off the controls Anita had on her burst. This would result in her systems overloading as Maria pumped petabytes of data into them. Or she could nix the system by reformating the hard drives or run a fragmentation protocol and destroy all the data.

In the end, the decision was made for her. Starbursting was messy but quicker to accomplish. Anita was moving fast, and Maria didn't have time to do anything fancy. She looped her program in just in time to prevent a feedback loop that would fry them both.

She could almost feel bad for Anita. Her last feed showed the monitors blinking, overloading with data. She could practically hear the hard drives filling up, the processors overheating— the horror when Anita realized what was happening— her frantic search for the fuse box. Everything went black.

Maria knew it was too little too late. By the time recognition of a starburst hitting your system occurred, it was too late to stop it. She began the arduous task of disassembling her connections to the infrastructure. She didn't want to leave any trace of her activities, and she had work to do. Real work.

Terminus awaited.

Chapter Twenty-Three

An End

Consequences were never a strong suit for Maria. She knew they existed, but they didn't apply to her. This should have been surprising. Most programmers were logic oriented. Each piece of code had logical outcomes. When they weren't what was expected, the flaw was in the programmer, not in the execution of the code. An unintended loop. A parameter that hadn't been set.

She'd lived her life cheating code. She was making it do what it wasn't intended to do. She cheated the system in every way she could. Even the greatest love of her life, Olivia, had been won at the cost of Olivia's new ex-girlfriend. Rules didn't apply to Maria.

The trend of the American government to constrict and control, to trample on citizens' liberties in the name of safety, didn't sit well with her. When people became more entranced by their electronic toys than by the well-being of their human counterparts, she saw the end of humanity. She saw the moment the new government had realized their method of control because it was also the moment she foretold the end of the world.

Within ten years, birth rates had dropped.

Protests were non-existent. Minorities were ghettoized and didn't realize it or care. The fantasies that they lived in were augmented versions of reality. Maria could run a model predicting the exact moment humanity wouldn't exist. Not really. They had been toying with uploading human consciousness into computer systems, becoming a living AI. Maria didn't think this counted. You weren't real unless you could kiss your wife, smell the air, and physically exist. Not that she did many of these things anymore.

Cosmic consequences she got. Personal ones, she did not.

Her world ended when she found out that Olivia had been executed. She was distilled into one action to implement: the Cause. To die a victorious martyr. There were no other options. No personal acts were left, just simple steps to reach her conclusion.

She hadn't expected Anita to visit her after frying her entire electronic infrastructure that had taken years to build. Therefore the jangle that broke her concentration on Terminus was unexpected. She went to the front counter in a daze, without checking her security monitors, without a thought to the contrary that Anita had come to yell at her.

"I know you're angry, but you'll understand I did it for your good," her words were ready. She quickly thought through a plan. Straight to the point seemed best. She wasn't in it to save the child's feelings or act as a punching bag. Get this over with and move on. Get back to her work.

"So glad you rationalized it," the voice was deeper than Anita's, older.

She looked up and froze— a mouse caught by the screech of an owl overhead. Move or freeze; the mouse was dead. One word slipped out, "Rose."

Rose's eyes were red-rimmed. She had a coldness that left no room for misinterpretation. She was middle-aged now, wrinkles etched into her face more of stress than outright age. She looked more like Olivia than ever. Her daughter had finally come.

"Maria Rose Gutierrez, I am done with you. I claim no kinship."

Rose bit the words off. Bitter as tannins, the words sucked the moisture from her mouth. She knew she'd harmed Anita by starbursting her system, but she didn't think it'd been this dastardly a move.

"It is good to see you," this may have been the wrong thing to say, but it was true. Rose had been a child when Maria was arrested. Rose had been a bright spot. A part of both Olivia and Maria, a continuation of their bond. Not someone she'd sought a relationship with, but someone she knew the world was better for having in it. She could almost imagine what Olivia looked like with Rose standing before her.

Rose moved forward and slapped a chip on the counter. It was nondescript. She stood there, her eyes drilling holes into Maria. She just stood there, watching her.

Maria picked up the chip, running a quick scan before sliding it into place. On her screen was a video image with a first-person perspective. She tapped the play button and let the video run.

"Goddess be damned, the bitch starburst me!" The words came in Anita's voice. Angry and hollow. As though she couldn't believe it but kicked herself for not seeing the possibility. Maria was familiar with that feeling when surrounded by melting and smoking systems. A lifetime of work gone. Her only satisfaction was that, in Anita's case, the feeling wouldn't be followed by the shrill sirens of a police force.

The camera panned left and right, taking the full measure of melted work. Anita stood up and walked into her living room. They no longer lived in the super clean dirty apartment. Instead, the living room was large. A comfy couch sat in front of a Holo projection VR display. Rose stood at a counter hitting buttons on the food printer for the thing. Anita went up and hugged Rose. There was some blurriness to the image. Maria assumed it was tears smudging up the contacts. The hug was long and desperate as the shock settled.

"I love you, Mom."

"I love you too, sweetie. Dinner should be done in ten minutes."

"Sounds good. I'm going to go for a quick walk."

Maria could tell that Rose caught the hollowness in Anita's voice. She saw her daughter think about saying something more, reaching out. She could only imagine how Anita might have responded to such an impulse. Rose let Anita be. Rose had no idea what had just happened but knew better than to kick the wasp nest.

"Make it quick," Rose could be heard calling

after her daughter as she walked out of the house.

Anita carefully closed the door behind her and took a deep breath. She walked, looking around. The video showed that her augmentation and network link was off. This girl didn't want to be found. She walked and walked. The air was cold. The empty city streets were lonely and grey. The slate buildings silently watched her walk along the sidewalk.

She paused momentarily, catching a glimpse of a raccoon tucking itself into a sewer. Beady eyes flashed at her as it cocked its head in her direction, cautiously considering her. An automated car flashed by.

She kept walking until she finally ended in the most beautiful part of the city. They had built a third bridge over the Mississippi during the green movement. When humans made one last grab at preventing the fifth extinction, they built a beautiful pedestrian bridge that spanned the mighty river for bikes and humans alike. Anita stood, watching the water. It was beautiful. All knew the water's toxicity levels were so high the water was undrinkable without risking a trip to the emergency room. Fish couldn't live in the water. If water birds hadn't gone extinct, they'd avoid it for the same reasons. It was the river Styx set into the side of a city.

Anita walked out into the middle of the bridge. Some mild foot traffic and a few bikes were her only company. Folks were finishing off their evening commute. Maria gasped when she saw Anita throw a leg over the railing.

"No, no, no, no, no," the words didn't stop Anita's second leg from going over the edge. She stood butt against the railing, a handgrip's release away from plunging 185 feet into the Mississippi.

"Oh goddess, please don't," Maria wanted to rip the chip out of her player. She didn't want to know what happened next. Maria didn't want to see this, didn't want to look this consequence in the eye. It would break her.

Then, to her surprise, Anita did the unexpected. She took a deep breath and turned around, clutching the metal railing and hugging it. She carefully threw a foot back over. She sat there straddling it, embracing it as though it was the only thing tethering her to life. She swung her other leg around and stepped back into the trail. Maria breathed a sigh of relief. Anita was panting with the emotion contemplating her death had brought up in her.

Maria had foreseen the lack of regard humans would develop for each other. Their fascination with augmentation and VR, the separation of reality and fiction. The commuter bike flew thirty miles an hour down the bridge when it clipped Anita's exhausted form. On the video feed, she couldn't see him. He was coming up from Anita's back. The whistle of the bike was audible. The crunching slap as it slammed into Anita— the crack of her neck.

The video feed twisted violently twisted around and went still. The view seemed to freeze on the Mississippi River sunset through the chainlink of the fence and Anita's unmoving foot. A voice overlay was heard as her chip connected to the emergency Network to call for medical assistance.

Maria let out a sob when the system reported there were no apparent life signs.

The video feed stopped. Maria ejected the chip. Rose was gone. Gone. A tear dripped down onto Maria's wrinkled hand, threatening the chip she clenched.

The front door jingled faintly.

Chapter Twenty-Four

Test Run

If the development of Terminus had been a Holo montage, it would be boring. It'd show a lonely woman sitting in a tiny room surrounded by computer monitors. A cat meanders around, causing mischief, and tries unsuccessfully to distract the woman from her work. Thankfully the cat was a virtual pet, or it would have died of starvation many years ago.

Technology leaped into minor sentience through the decades. Computer-based intelligence was predictive, then generative, then wholly adaptive. It developed programs, realities, and other AIs. This is how Olivia and Maria gained so much notoriety as hackers. They had an AI army at their beck and call. AI development had been Maria's specialty, and Olivia had recruited her to execute some of her more ambitious plans. The government had its AIs lurking in the system, protecting the critical infrastructure and the military networks. It took an army to defeat an army.

When Maria was released from jail, she'd found a few of her old AIs still operating on the Dark Net. Some had just continued on their base programming, developing minor AIs that could perform Network infiltrations. Some did the equivalent of banging their head against a wall, muttering in a corner. Suffice it to say she walked into a pretty sophisticated environment. The infiltration AIs had done what they do, penetrating the Network. Some were caught, but most weren't. They had no human consciousness directing them, so they moved with a robotic grace. Observers could track no patterns. The intelligence wasn't going after a specific target. They followed the last command given- saturate the Network. They became static on the line.

By Maria's calculation, they'd infiltrated most of North America, including several military complexes. In effect, they could open back door access to any infected hub nearly at will. At first, she used this power sparingly, as she didn't want to be detected. This infrastructure, created without formal direction, was the backbone of Terminus.

One other relic of her former life had survived. Her love story with Olivia transcended the physical and emotional. They'd created a flesh and blood child, but they'd also made a virtual child. Their most sophisticated AI had survived.

Olivia had long ago named it Significant, a designation meant to make it stand apart from its peers. The AI was significant. It could operate without any direction and sometimes had a will of its own, not unlike an unruly teenager. For this reason, and a few others, they hadn't equipped the program with much ability to interact with humans. The dangers and consequences of making it genuinely aware of its nature and that of its creators were a risk they hadn't been willing to take.

Ultimately, the world can be ended in multiple ways. Humans had made a good start already with the mass extinctions, the acidic atmosphere, and the melted ice caps. Populations had decreased from unnatural mother nature events. The advent of the globalization of technology availability virtually ended war, but it also led to a sharp decrease in birth rates as the need for physical human interaction plummeted. Zoos were barren, people interacted through virtual avatars, and nutrient-infused food cubes were the status quo. Nobody cared. Well, almost nobody.

She discovered a fringe paramilitary organization in Kansas. Paramilitary organizations were popular 100 years ago. When the Regime change was looming, folks thought they had something worthwhile for the government to take. It turned out the government was just interested in placating everyone, letting them go to sleep.

The Free Staters, however, hung around. They were descendants of farmers. They still worked in hydroponic fields growing nutrients to provide the base of food cubes, but deep down, they remembered the waving wheat of their ancestors. Her initial plan needed conspirators. Someone had to physically plant a link to Significant into the military complex mainframe. Surprisingly, the mainframe resided in a Military Network Hub outside a Public Network Hub in Topeka, Kansas.

The other hubs were one in Tacoma, another in the Pentagon, and a third in Monterey, California. They were all heavily fortified, defended, just like the Topeka complex. The main difference was the Free Staters. They'd worked on infiltrating the Topeka complex for years, figuring it would be the linchpin of any activity central to their operations. Not that they had a plan. They were fighting for simple survival.

The Terminus montage should have included a Mission Impossible-style attack on the Topeka complex. However, it was much simpler than that. Ed, the son of Steve and Regina, was a tenth-generation Kansan. He had a Native heritage that extended down into the very bones of the land.

Ed worked a desk job as a minor developer in charge of the facilities website in the defense department. Ed went to work, sat at a computer, and plugged in a USB chip. The alarms that should have gone off were silenced so quickly that no one would realize something had happened until the system monitors looked over the Network access logs at the end of the week.

Ed had given notice to return to the farm and help his ailing parents. Even those that looked at the access logs didn't notice the significance of the error at 10:21 AM on Nov 1st. It was a blip, probably a power flicker due to a storm. Didn't it storm on Monday? Significant was in, and no one could stop Maria now.

Chapter Twenty-Five

Topeka

Maria's response to despair had always been to throw herself into work, which is why jail had been so hard. There was only so much a person could do with a three-by-six living space. For three of those years, she'd been stuck with a cellmate on suicide watch, which meant she couldn't have any writing instrument in the cell itself. She'd had to manically write letters to Anita on scraps of paper at lunch.

Anita's death hit her hard. She wasn't close to the child. She barely registered as a person. In jail, Anita had been her repository. She was the hope that one day her program would be whole. She was also the future for which she was creating Terminus and, hopefully, Omega. The waste of Anita's death was appalling. Anita had a future, and she was good at technological manipulation. She was a lot like Maria. She was of Maria. She was the last connection outside of Rose to humanity, to her Olivia.

Emotionally she was a survivor. She'd survived the purge. She'd survived imprisonment. She'd survived emotional and physical abuse by her captors. Maria survived the death of everything that meant something to her. Anita lost a program and contemplated jumping off a bridge. She then had the audacity to fail at living. It was incomprehensible.

Maria would never get Rose back. Intellectually she'd known Rose had walked away from her 40 years ago. Maria had taken Rose's mother and now her daughter. Nothing, nothing could bring her back. Nothing could bring Olivia or Anita back. She had no family, only the plan. She was distilled and burned down to the mission. Maria almost fooled herself into thinking that that was it.

A spark flickered to life. When one is dying of thirst in the desert, it's easy to grasp the faintest hope. The urge to crawl toward the oasis is irresistible, even if it's a known mirage.

She continued working on her program but also started tracking Rose. She'd set several Network watches on her daughter. The only solution she could see was to show Rose the truth about the government. How it was slowly killing everyone, how it was the cause of Olivia's death. How technology's all-consuming power over people was causing them irreparable harm, even death.

How it was causing environmental destruction. The poisoned seas, the empty parks, the extinctions.

Rose had moved to Kansas. Probably to spite Maria. She knew Maria didn't like traveling. She had never wanted to be outside of her city. Like many technophiles, she exhibited a tendency towards agoraphobia. Jail had been her foray into the world, and it hadn't made a great impression.

There was no way she would attempt to visit Rose in Kansas, and Rose knew it. Maria copied some code from her program and made a low-grade, self-improving AI to follow her daughter. She'd check in on them daily, trying to influence her daughter in passive and active ways.

The deviant down the street had a Network Error that exposed his personal Network to the public. Her daughter's neighborhood was subjected to the man's fantasies on the block for a week before the administrators figured out how to turn it off. The event made the news, and the man was arrested. The "Nude Infection" was labeled as a Network error, not a malicious event. They couldn't figure out how it happened, so they shrugged their shoulders and moved on.

For a week straight, every time her daughter tried to watch a movie on the Network, the AI implanted dystopia movies in her top 5 choices. The type where technology takes over the world, where big brother is watching, discovering the truth about Soylent Green. She observed her daughter swearing off protein cubes for a week. Each little victory felt like a triumph.

Maria made life uncomfortable in little ways. The auto-drive function on the car would go out. The Smart features that allowed her house settings to be adjusted by voice command stopped responding to Rose's voice. Her chip burnt out. It was the year of technological hell for Rose. Little unsubtle hints that not all was right with technology.

It took that year for Maria to finish her work. She'd had three projects going. The first one was set to convince Rose of the need for Maria's end solution. The second project she worked on was to unleash a virus on the government system to execute an EMP pulse within America's borders, an Omega event. Terminus would be a test of the end solution. The thread Ed planted on the Military Network Hub would slowly infiltrate the American military.

The third was working out a transfer protocol. She'd built an improving, evolving AI program. The plan was to transfer a personality chip into the AI. Then the EMP program could be run throughout the Network, allowing for a nationwide outage. The prospect was both terrifying and invigorating. That particular program would nix all Network activities and weaken the government. It would effectively put her out of business as well.

She'd chosen Topeka as her test ground primarily because of Rose. With success, Rose would have to admit that Maria was right. She knew the time was coming. Her daughter had ordered an emergency food supply. The "Never-ending Artic Story" got to her. These were the little ways the government manipulated people. She'd just stolen some of their code to do it to her daughter. Instead of getting fed the propaganda generated by the government machine, Rose was getting what Maria wanted her to see.

This power didn't bother Maria. It never had. She owned her power and wielded it unflinchingly. She refused to contemplate morality when getting shot at in a war for civilization. She acted.

So on November 14th, a Sunday, Maria hit the execute button on her code. It took two hours for the virus to worm into the missile silo in northwest Kansas. It took 10 minutes to break down the firewall structured to keep intrusions out of the Military Network. Four minutes for her virus to race through the military installation and 25 seconds to program the EMP missile. It sent her back a confirmation request. This was the one potential flaw in the program, the one way they could trace the act back to her. She thought it was necessary, though, one final check on the execution.

She didn't hesitate. She typed in her password, "Anita," and hit enter. The next instant, the missile launched. Two minutes later, it detonated over Kansas, bringing down the Network.

Her plan had the flaw all her dreams had. She hadn't anticipated the unintended consequences. Kansas went dark in a moment, a blink of an eye. With its darkness, so went the central corridor, as Kansas had been the Network hub to the north and south. It was an unassuming link to the center of the entire country.

The government's watch programs were not nearly as sophisticated as Maria would have guessed. When Kansas dropped off the Network, they assumed the Free Staters had gained state control, which was partially true.

Maria had used the organization as a front for much of her activity. They had willingly helped her infiltrate several bases, Military Networks and knew of her overall plans. The Free Staters were determined to be a part of the revolution. They were technophobes with guns who had no real impact on the government in any reliable way. Until they met

Maria, she used them to penetrate several bases. Their organization became more prominent with her help. Maria wasn't the only one to lose a loved one in the fight.

The central administration feared the worst and quickly decided that if Kansas didn't play by the rules, they wouldn't be allowed to play. They launched forces meant to exterminate and damage the land. It was a total war on their own people.

It happened quickly and was all hush-hush to the rest of the country. Network activity had ceased in Kansas, so they bombed the state without fear of retribution. Topeka, being the capital, was their primary target. However, no major city in the state stood unscathed when they were done.

The government erected a virtual, and later, a physical wall along the Kansan border. It was meant to keep out reporters and rebels.

It was justifiable in Maria's eyes. If a person were shooting at her, she'd shoot back. Survival was about action.

Yet again, she'd betrayed her own.

Chapter Twenty-Six

Ash and Bone

The news hit in less than 24 hours. Their news. The headlines scrolled across her interface, "Kansan Capital Destroyed by Rebels," "Topeka No More," and "Free State Terrorists Destroy Kansas Network." The headlines all pointed to terrorist activity in Kansas that destroyed it. Worse, they had used radioactive weapons in retribution, and the fall-out would impact the environment for thousands of years. Tens of thousands had lost their lives instantly in Topeka, and millions would be losing their lives over time.

Maria was frantic. She had to find out if Rose had made it. She tried to infiltrate Kansas electronically in any way she could. The problem was accessible electronics didn't exist in Kansas. The only active Network in that area was the military fly-over vehicles and unmanned drones. She worked for a week to take over a drone. It had to be untraceable, which was hard on the Military Net without Free Stater intervention. She ended up getting in through a Captain's ill-thought password. The mission was quick. She'd taken control of package delivery drones before. Military surveillance ones weren't much different.

Two hours and, she was in Kansas airspace. She went directly to Topeka. The government had set up satellite connections since the ground signals were fried. Maria had only as long as it took for them to figure out that they had a rogue drone on their hands. They could sever the data connection, and she'd be done.

Thankfully, the drone zipped into Topeka unimpeded. Maria used the onboard GPS program to pinpoint her daughter's house. The neighborhood had taken heavy damage, as it was just outside the total blast zone of the bomb. Maria immediately realized that although Rose might still be alive, it was likely she'd be affected by the radiation. The drone buzzed in front of the house, cameras swiveling. Did a curtain shift? She used the zoom function. Nothing. She realized the drone was equipped with infrared and toggled the switch over.

The unmistakable outline of a woman's heat signature was shown in the window.

"Rose," the word slipped out, a small hope. She moved the drone closer, trying to capture a standard light photo. If she was going to risk going into Topeka, she had to ensure it was her daughter. The image clicked.

As she brought it up on her screen, the drone went dead. They'd discovered her.

It didn't matter, however, as the picture showed the clear lines on Rose's face. Maria was going to plan a trip to Kansas. She began doing some research. She had money. That wasn't a problem. The trick was to procure the right equipment without making anyone suspicious. She needed an ancient vehicle that could be driven without Network access. She needed radioactive protective clothing. She needed supplies, maps, and a plan to get over the border.

The government had announced that to prevent a flood of refugees, disease, and terrorism from invading; a fence was erected as though Kansans had given up their citizenship. Construction had begun and would be done within a month. This incredible feat was to be accomplished by the government using autonomous robotic machinery that could chop wood, cut it into fencing, and lay it. Highly productive, the robots did not have to sleep.

This was her in. Robots like this had to be Networked to work together. Anything Networked could be hacked. Instead of shutting them down, however, she inserted a few more directions. A couple of entry points that hadn't been in the original plans. It would require them to dig out small tunnels under the fence and reinforce these culverts with piping.

The beauty of automated systems was that they were trusted to do their job independently. No one questioned the tunnels. They just assumed it was per spec. Complacency was a double-edged sword. Maria now had a way into the border. The closest tunnel was several miles north of Kansas City. She'd bought an old-school motorcycle. She hadn't ridden one in years but figured it was like riding a bike. You never really forgot.

For all the programming and thought that went into her tunnel through the wall and her route to Kansas, Maria still had trouble leaving her house.

The service delivered the old-school motorcycle to her door. It sat right next to the overgrown bush blocking the store entrance. The bike was shiny and old. It'd been outfitted with automated riding functions while retaining its manual controls. The thing would work here and in Kansas.

Maria paused. The thought of traveling under the sky. The unlimited nature of air and space and the universe. It made her chest tighten.

What have I come to?

The question wouldn't go away. Her need to get to Rose was fierce. She took small steps out from the eaves of the store, loading the motorcycle with the necessary supplies: food packets, first aid, rain gear, and printouts of maps.

Take care of our daughter.

Olivia's last words bubbled in her mind. She could do this. She'd done a crappy job so far, but she could do *this*. She swung one leg slowly over the two-wheeled beast and kicked the engine on. A visual display popped up, asking for a location to travel to. She clicked some buttons. She would deal with her fear on their way to Columbia. Take control later.

Before Maria gave it another thought, the motorcycle started moving. She hugged the beast with her legs, put a death grip on the handlebars, and concentrated on breathing. Don't look up, and it'll all be okay.

The cycle turned onto an on-ramp to the main thoroughfare to Kansas City. There was no traffic. People didn't travel much anymore. The bike kicked into high gear, and she felt bubbling deep in her gut. The wind whipped past her face and pulled at her jacket. She was free. A whoop escaped her mouth. Excitement won the battle over fear for a moment.

Her passage through the tunnel was uneventful. She wasn't sure how far the Network extended past the fence, but it couldn't be far. She slowly made her way forward on the Kansan road, looking around for hints that anything was different.

"Where are you going?" a woman's voice cut through the bramble. Maria was never one to like admitting defeat or surprise. She went with honesty.

"I'm headed to Topeka. I've got to find my daughter."

A woman stepped out behind a bush. Her face was full of ropey, raw wounds. It was as though half of it had melted off. That might be exactly what had happened. The woman stood squarely, though, full of pride.

"You don't want to go to Topeka. There's nothing left."

"There is. I saw her."

The woman didn't have much ability to stretch her damaged face into an expression. However, she managed disbelief pretty well, "How? How could you have possibly been to Topeka?"

Maria hesitated, giving the lie away. She didn't know whether she should admit to hijacking the drone to this woman.

"I hijacked a military drone and dropped it in front of my daughter's house in NOTO."

NOTO, she knew, was shorthand for North Topeka. She hoped the slang would connect her to the area enough that the woman would believe her.

"It's possible North Topeka was out of the blast zone, but it's in the radiation shadow. Even if she was alive after the bomb, chances are she isn't now."

"I have to try."

The woman nodded, "I understand. I'll let you pass, but you've got to come back to Lost Ranch, 2 miles West of this entrance. The border guard here will not let you pass until you have a chit from Ed. Tell them Natalie sent you."

Only then did Maria see the rifle leaning against the tree next to the woman and the pistol on her belt.

"Understood. Where are you from, Natalie?"

The woman looked at her, eyes almost dead in the fading light, "I'm one of the few survivors of Lawrence." Maria shivered. Lawrence was twenty-five minutes from Topeka. Could anyone survive?

Maria nervously saluted the hollowed-out woman, revved the motor, and began speeding along the county road, heading West toward Topeka. Her thoughts trailed behind her on the road. She hadn't thought about the possibility that Rose would be dead or dying when she arrived. Radiation shadows were not within her purview of knowledge. She felt blind without a tie to the Network. She carried a printout of maps and directions, as GPS wasn't reliable in the dead zone. Overall the trip was quiet. No one was on the roads. Likely none of the vehicles worked at all. She heard the pop of a gun only once, probably some survivor thinking she was government.

She took the county roads into Topeka to avoid being on an exposed highway. The streets on the outskirts of the city were barren. Some of the stores had been looted. It looked like an apocalyptic wasteland. The art district was deserted. Likely, everyone had been fleeing the fallout.

She turned into her daughter's neighborhood. All of the augmentation had been taken off of the buildings. Even so, it wasn't too bad. Only a couple of houses looked abandoned. She pulled up to the house and cut the motor. The drone she'd been using sat dead in the front yard, its metallic black coat making it look particularly frightening. A viper ready to spring. She tried to shake the unease it gave her. Instead, she took a moment to top off her tank with the extra gas she'd brought and headed to the front door with the extra anti-radiation suit she'd bought.

Her knock rang hollowly in the house. She followed up with a shout, "Rose, are you in?" No answer.

Maria wasn't going to be able to kick open the door, she wasn't in very good shape, and her legs already ached from the bike ride. Instead, she went to the one-car garage. With the electricity off, it likely clicked over to manual release. With a hard tug on the handle, the garage door slid open.

"Push it down! Push it down!" Rose screeched at her, running forward and slamming the door shut behind Maria. Overwhelming relief and a release of guilt gripped Maria momentarily until her daughter turned around.

Rose stood, eyes blinking at her, trying to

comprehend who had invaded her space. Her hair had begun to fall out in large splotches, red weeping lesions covered her arms, and her skin was pale, beyond white.

"Don't you know the metal protects from the radiation? Why did you lift it?" Rose was still babbling. Maria kept her helmet on. She wasn't sure she wanted Rose to know who she was, why she was here.

"Put this on," Maria said, muffled through her helmet, "I'm here to take you to the recovery camp."

"You're here to save me? Are you really here? I saw the drone and thought someone might come by, but then it died in the yard," Rose began putting on the jacket, slipping on the pants. She took the spare helmet and pulled it on. She didn't notice as a significant strand of hair fell out as she locked it in place.

"How far?" came Rose's now muffled question.

"30-40 minutes. Are you okay to hold on?"

Rose nodded. She was sick but had a little bit of kick left. They mounted the bike and settled in. Maria wondered if Rose had held on so long because of the drone and if she inadvertently prolonged her suffering by giving her hope in a hopeless situation. The motor roared to life, a welcome end to all conversation.

Rose clutched her tight and, at one instance, leaned forward, cheek against her back. Maria let go for a while, just drove, and enjoyed the closeness she'd never been able to experience with Rose. This was her own flesh and blood. The last breath of

Olivia in the world. The thoughts of what could have been tumbled through her head, debris tipping over the edge of a waterfall, slipping off of rocks and stones. Some thoughts continued downstream, and others were wedged in, unable to move. Unable to give her relief. An image of Anita slipped in, the talented granddaughter she'd never get to know. Of the life she could have had with Olivia and Rose. Of the time she'd spent in jail thinking about how to end the world, not how to save her daughter. Of how she was going to tell Rose who she was.

She pulled to a stop at a crossroads close to where she imagined Ed's ranch was located. Pulling out a paper map, she scanned for a likely suspect.

Rose pulled in close, her words putting a bramble in Maria's throat, "Don't worry, I know I'm dying. I just wanted to say thank you for saving me and for taking me away from that place. I'd rather die somewhere out here, in the sunlight. Thank you for coming to get me."

Maria spotted a likely spot for the ranch on the map. Through her tears, she revved the motor and took off. Rose clutched her even tighter as though her unacknowledged thanks could creep into the mystery driver through her grip. They bounced and jangled. It couldn't be comfortable for Rose, but they had no choice. It was move Rose now or let her die where she was.

Finally, they arrived at the farm, the motorcycle's headlight playing over an old horse barn.

"Halt!" cried a gruff voice. A solidly built man in overalls stepped out from behind old farm equipment. A loader? A harvester? He held a shotgun in his hand and eyed her suspiciously.

She cut the engine, kept her hands out, flipped up the visor, "Natalie sent me to talk to Ed."

The man sauntered up, wearing cowboy boots and jeans with several worn holes. His t-shirt was dusty and sweat-soaked. As he stepped into the light, she stifled a gasp. All of his exposed skin was a raw red rash. She kept her eyes on his face trying to look as non-threatening as possible. Rose sagged exhaustedly against the motorcycle, just waiting for the exchange to be over.

"Natalie sent me from the border. I've got Rose here. She needs help."

The man walked closer, eying them both, "Alright, follow me."

She turned to help Rose up and forgot. She'd forgotten for a moment that Rose hated her, that this was her fault, that Rose didn't know she was responsible for her rescue.

Rose gasped, "You!" she screeched in her pathetic voice, "You?! You caused this. This is your fault." Maria's daughter finally realized precisely who her heroine was. She knew without a question that it had been Maria's fault.

Rose scrabbled backward away from Maria as though she was about to get attacked. Rose freaked out and was close to collapsing in her weakened state. Maria froze, not knowing what to do.

The man with the shotgun stepped forward. He snagged her arm, "Hold this," to her surprise 'this' was his shotgun. He slowly walked towards Rose as though approaching a frightened animal. Maria supposed she was, frightened and hurt. Rose was hyperventilating. The man hurried between them, and Rose's breathing calmed slightly.

"It's okay little bird," his voice was rough but kind. Maria should have been surprised, but she wasn't. This man exuded trust. She took the hint and turned, walking to the faint glow of the farmhouse. It was time to meet Ed in person.

Chapter Twenty-Seven

Ed

Ed was larger than life. Maria knew exactly who he was as soon as she entered the barn. He stood a commanding six foot eight. He had the lean build of a farmer's boy and met the physical specifications of the *jrocked profile,* her contact for the Free Staters.

"Ed, I presume," she stepped towards him, hand extended.

He smoothed over his surprise by extending his hand, "I presume we've met?" His voice made it evident that he doubted this statement.

"You're the Free State leader," she said frankly. Her online chats with the man highlighted his directness, so she went with it.

"You have me at a disadvantage," his statement ended as Rose was carried into the barn. She had both her arms around the man's neck, giving him a look of adoration as though he'd braved the radiated zone to save her.

A flurry of activity and Rose was set on a table. A woman who appeared to be a doctor began an examination. Maria looked away, knowing what the result of the examination was going to be.

Ed watched her, calculating, "Maria. You're

Maria, and that is your daughter you were trying to save." Maria didn't realize she'd shared so much in her collaboration with the Free Staters, "Yes, your face says it all— hot dog with mustard on top. You guys, this is Maria!! The Maria!!"

Several people gathered around, patting her on the back. A couple of people thanked her with tears in their eyes. One man gave her a fierce hug.

Another contingent of people stood apart. They muttered in quiet voices. Maria paid them no mind. She noticed that many of those that stood apart were burned or hurt. This was unsurprising given the nature of what had happened here. She was both heroine and villain.

Ed took her arm and led her away from the well-wishers. He took her to a corner of the barn with picnic tables and an obvious mess tent. She sat down, thankful and weary from the day's events.

"We need your help," Ed babbled quietly.

"You had my help. I did this," Maria waved at it all.

Ed's smile was pained with a tinge of forbearance. Maria didn't like it.

"We are a week away from starving. Kansas is, Kansas is ruined. Half the people here have lost half of their families, and everyone else lost *someone*. Only a few people know how close we are to starvation. I haven't had the heart to ration. There's no point. What can we do?"

"How can you thank me? You're a forkful away from starvation."

His desperation was apparent. Maria couldn't help the thought: *but you asked for this, you wanted it.*

"You and I both know we asked for this. To blame you for the result, people will do it, but they shouldn't. Some see you as a hero now, but when folks start starving, you will be infamous. I flipped the switch as much as you."

She tried to feel something. Pity? Compassion? They'd worked together to bring the ruin to fruition. It wasn't her fault if they hadn't planned better. Her gaze, however, found the form of Rose. Hell was paved with these decisions.

"I'll help. You have to take care of her," she motioned to her daughter. She was surrounded by a small group, still getting medical attention.

"You know…" his voice petered off. *You know she's walking dead. You know she's poisoned beyond recovery. You know she only has a few days, a week at most.*

"I know. I can't help but want her final days to be at peace. They wouldn't be around me."

"You're leaving?"

"Yes, expect the first delivery in three days by drone at the border culvert. I will keep you alive and give you a start, but you will have to figure out a way to make your way in the world. Grow kale, grow potatoes."

"What are potatoes?"

"I've read about them. They're good mashed," he nodded, pretending to understand.

She stood up, "Take care of my daughter."

"We would have anyway. You know that. This seems like a small price for us to pay for sustainment."

"Don't thank me, Ed. You may have been naive about what the Free Stater's agenda would produce. I was much less so. This is something I need to do. If nothing else, I owe it to Rose. She found a home here in Kansas."

She looked him in the eye and extended her hand. He shook it, tall, strong, ready to lead his people. She took one last look at Rose on the table. One last look then walked out of the barn towards her bike. She moved stiffly. Her knees ached. Her heart ached. She was getting too old.

Chapter Twenty-Eight

Time

Maria wouldn't have classified it as suicide. That did not accurately describe her activity. She had worked with the Free Staters for three years to get them set up. She'd sent them food, seeds, supplies, books, and potatoes by uncrewed vehicle and drone. She'd worked hard to get the survivors on their feet and her plans in place.

The EMP had worked. The reaction of the government had been the problem. However, now that the Kansans were on their feet, it was evident that humanity would survive. The Free Staters could lead the way with techniques that hadn't been implemented in a century.

The other hope she had was looking at the overall population of America. Folks weren't connecting like they used to. The only ones interested in kids were the fundamentalists and the gays. She and Olivia had been a part of the trend themselves. With populations lower, she could see a future.

The problem was, she could also see the future she'd created for Anita and Rose.

The future was constantly in flux. Technology progressed. She'd developed a Calibrated Heuristic

Reciprocal Interactive Synthetic, CHRIS. Chris was an AI that operated in Augmented Plus Reality. She was loaded with history, fake family, house, and job. She even had a cat that gave her comfort. Synthetic Augmentation was a burgeoning field. A normal SA AI would do all the functions one might expect of the help. Only they'd do it for your augmented reality. Code tended to drift, and neighborhoods would degrade. SA AIs could program, have complex thoughts and intervene. They could participate in life like a family member or float around like a ghost.

Maria was particularly proud of Chris, though. She was independent, and Maria had worked out a way for her to operate completely unknowing of her nature. She would interact with her environment in natural patterns. The programming would pick up on the environment and alter her awareness to make it interactive. To create individuals when needed. Her background included an ex and a few absent children.

By the time CHRIS was done, Maria had to add some programming that prevented her from interacting with actual humans unless they were predefined. This was due to some new laws concerning SA AIs, some of which had gone rogue when their elderly owners had died. Folks were unable to tell who was real and who wasn't. CHRIS was keyed only to her and was set to Maria's bio-monitor.

Maria kept Anita's personal chip. It held her entire life's data on it, nearly from inception. When bought, chips were connected to external memory storage devices. They came with a standard year or two of service, then were pay-to-use afterward. This encouraged folks to upgrade. The storage was pretty pricey. The chips monitored everything about a person, from health and brain waves to visual and audio perception. No one had thought about it yet, but chips became imbued with an imprint of a person's life, personality, and thoughts.

Maria had thought about it long and hard. CHRIS was her prototype for a SA AI for Anita's imprint. However, the load didn't work since so much of Anita's being was wrapped up as a flesh and blood person. Maria immediately scrapped the idea, instead focusing on making CHRIS more lifelike.

She worked on plan B for Anita. Maria was never one to exhibit emotion. However, her intensity on the program was a good indication of her feelings about it. Everything was cut a little short. Life tends to do that for those who expect too much of it. She'd been programming, programming, programming. She'd developed several algorithms to help her program. Several minor AIs were working on different aspects of the overall system.

Her monitor started going off. She axed the alarm and kept going. An hour later, the sharp jangle of the store door woke her from the trance of screens. She tried to jump up but swayed to the side. She had to leave her technology lab. What was wrong with her legs?

She stumbled, numb. Her fingers ached. Was the heat even on? It was cold. She could hear someone calling her name.

"Maria? Maria, where are you?"

She had to get out of her hidden room. She stumbled to the door, pulling it closed behind her. The panel clicked and locked. It was safe. She collapsed.

"I'm up here," her voice sounded feeble to herself. There was so much left to do. She hadn't loaded more than a few years of history into Chris. Anita's program didn't have anything from the fall of Kansas forward. There wasn't time. She found some strength. It wasn't time yet. Her voice was louder this time. "I'm up here."

"She's over here, Tom."

Two sets of feet creaked up the stairs. Maria was aware of them but couldn't talk. It was as though her tongue was swollen. She'd be worried, anxious. It was fitting that the project she'd worked on her entire life would end as she approached the finish line.

"Ma'am, we need to take you to the hospital. Are you still with us?"

Maria couldn't respond. The world was going dark.

"I don't think she's conscious, Tom."

"Yeah."

She existed in twilight. She felt them tip her onto a bodyboard and carry her to the waiting ambulance her health monitor summoned. She felt the jostle of the ambulance as it sped to the local hospital. She heard the doctor ordering tests for the nurses to perform. She remembered them lifting her hand to scan her chip for identifying information.

"Go ahead and dose her. We need her to sleep.

There's no head trauma, and she's not having a stroke, so we're safe. She should wake up in a few hours." *But I am awake*. Her thoughts weren't getting through.

She could feel the IV feeding her liquids, a nurse injected something into the stream, and Maria was entirely out.

She woke feeling swollen. The IV had been feeding her liquids for hours. She felt energetic, ready to move. This proved difficult as she was tied down to the bed.

"Help," a raspy voice called out. It was her voice, "Help!"

Nobody came. She tried to move, but the restraints had her locked in place. She did what she could, looking around. The antiseptic hospital room was white and clean. Metal rails surrounded her with brown leather straps tight around her arms and legs. Panic set in, and she strained against the restraints.

She'd been in the hospital twice in jail and spent both times in a sterile white room slightly smaller than this one. The leather bit into her arms and legs. She lifted her head and looked down. Her panicked breathing slowed. She was old. This wasn't jail. She wasn't in prison, hadn't been incarcerated for decades. She was Maria Rose Gutierrez. She would be okay.

In her calm state, a nurse didn't take too long to check on her. They had a 30-minute check.

"How are you doing, Miss Maria," the nurse spoke, not expecting an answer. Maria had been lying there, thinking of code with her eyes closed, thinking of the next steps. What did she have to finish versus what she could strip out?

"Not so hot," Maria croaked, scaring the nurse.

The woman jumped, her dark skin standing out in contrast to the light room.

"So you are back with the living then?" the woman asked, "I'm guessing you're thirsty."

Maria nodded. Her throat was dry, and it was hard to talk.

The woman immediately unstrapped her wrists, "Apologies for the restraints. You kept trying to pull the IV out and fell out of bed at least once."

Maria guessed that was forgivable. She rubbed her wrists. They were sore but not raw.

"Here, I will undo your legs. Stay in bed, and I'll get some water for you."

Maria nodded again. Now that she was awake and less panicky, she wasn't about to rip out the IV and run out of the hospital room. They'd taken out her chip, and she was virtually blind. She didn't even know which hospital she was in.

The nurse did as promised and left to get some water. Maria had decided to keep quiet until she was back. She tried to sit up, but the effort made her dizzy. The room spun.

"Maria, please be careful. You are still recovering," the woman's voice was lightly accented.

She wasn't going to argue with the nurse. Her spinning head was keeping her still. A paper cup was pressed into her hand. She brought it to her lips, and the cold water soothed her mouth. Maria drank it all slowly, unable to stop. The ice chips melted on her tongue.

"Thank you," she got out, handing the cup back only to have it replaced by another, which she savored slowly. The cold made her head refocus. Questions began to swim in her head, "Why am I here? What's wrong with me?"

"You had extremely low blood pressure due to multiple reasons. Your bio-monitor alerted the paramedics, which is a good thing. You passed out at the top of the stairs when they arrived."

Maria nodded that correlated with her memory, but there was something else, "But why was my blood pressure so low?"

Silence for a moment, "That's something that'd be better coming from the doctor. She's due back in thirty minutes for her rounds. I will say that you were extremely dehydrated. You need to take better care of yourself."

Maria carefully nodded, "I'm still feeling lightheaded."

"That should pass later today. We're still working on rehydrating you, and your blood pressure should be higher. I'm going to get you some more water," Maria had finished her second cup, "and you should drink as long as you're still thirsty. After the doctor's visit, we'll see about dinner."

She lightly patted Maria on the leg, giving her an 'I'll be right back look.'

Maria waited. She evaluated herself. Her hip was sore, probably from the fall. She did feel thirsty, dreadfully thirsty. She wondered why she hadn't felt that before. The IV itched. Overall she didn't feel too bad.

"Miss Gutierrez, correct?" a white coat entered the room with a tablet.

She swallowed. Her throat was still sore, "Yes."

"Good. Alright, so we've got two treatment plans for you. We can put you on chemotherapy, prolonging your life and possibly putting you in remission. Life expectancy with chemotherapy is twelve to eighteen months. I will warn you that it will not be pleasant. Do you have family that can assist?"

She was too old. She'd outlived her family. She answered the doctor with a negative shake of the head.

"Then you might want to consider another option. We do not have a gene therapy that will push this aggressive cancer into remission. However, a meta-neutralizer is available. The cancer will take its course within six months. However, the meta-neutralizer therapy will neutralize most symptoms and give you the best end-of-life experience possible."

"I have cancer?"

The doctor looked up from her tablet, "The nurse didn't tell you? Obviously not. Miss Gutierrez, I'm sorry, but you have an aggressive hybrid lung cancer. Your records here say that you were incarcerated at La Quienz Federal Penitentiary. This disease has been commonly reported by released inmates from that location. We have not been able to pinpoint a cause."

I have cancer.

"Is there someone we can call for you?"

"No," she'd killed everyone in her life that might have been there for her, "No, I do not have any living family."

"That's unfortunate. Is there anything we can do for you?"

"When do you need a decision?"

The woman looked at her, evaluating a response, "The sooner we know, the sooner we can begin treatment, the more effective it will be."

So now, she had to begin treatment now. Fuck cancer.

Chapter Twenty-Nine

End of the Line

She was between worlds, fragmented. The doctor had left her with very little choice. Chemotherapy with a side of radiation had a meager chance of working out and a very high chance of spending the rest of her days in a cancer ward. With no one at home to help her, they wouldn't let her go home, not alone. She couldn't continue her work with a nursemaid. Even an AI nursemaid would figure out she was up to something illegal.

Meta-neutralizer therapy was it. But her project timeline extended out at least five more years. How do you fit five years into six months? Into a month? She was injected with the therapy treatment later that afternoon. The effect was almost immediate, between the IV of fluids hydrating her to levels her body had never experienced and the therapy hitting the pain centers of her brain. She felt buoyed.

She was discharged later in the night. They gave her a small gray case of syringes. Seven doses over seven days, and it would be done. Whatever life-extending ability therapy could give her would be racing through her bloodstream. What could she accomplish in seven days? The old texts claimed God made the world in seven days. Could she destroy it?

Upon getting home, she immediately enacted her brick program, which shut down the shop front, changing the augmented appearance into a solid wall. She didn't want a hint of a chance of a customer coming in. Rose had been her last visitor.

She walked up the stairs slowly. Her knees still ached. Damn, meta-neutralizer therapy couldn't cure old age. Not yet, at least. She typed her password on the panel and waited as the door slid open.

The room was muted. It had entered rest mode after not being consulted for four hours. However, the programs were wired to the door, so the holographic projectors sent an image of her VR pet, Tanda, walking over to greet her.

"Good evening Tanda," the words were silly, but they helped her. She'd bought the VR pet program several years back when she'd discovered she hadn't talked in a month. Tanda gave her a reason to speak but didn't require conversation in return.

The cat gave a tiny appreciative mew in response. It began to purr as it pretended to brush up against Maria's legs. At that moment, she had the answer.

She'd long ago decided to embrace her Frankensteinian thoughts after Anita died. After the Kansas disaster, she knew she'd never be able to execute Omega. It'd been done for years. She couldn't get up the nerve. Instead, she'd been working on a chip transfer of Anita's saved base personality, preferences, and life to an AI matrix. It had to be sophisticated enough to handle the complete essence of a fully functioning human.

She'd decided that since Anita's life had been cut short because of Maria's actions, giving Anita as much life as she could made sense. That life was coming very quickly to an end. Maria had used the work done on brain wave modulation and chip control. She'd made a system where Anita's residual personality would override Maria's. However, her problem was the dissonance between her 75-year-old body and her granddaughter's 18-year-old psyche. She'd breached some issues by inputting memories of the last 15 years: historical events, basic back story. Anita, reborn, would have most of the clues she needed to interact with the world. The only problem was that she'd see Maria's face when she looked in a mirror.

"Have you ever read Frankenstein?" the significant part of CHRIS's AI asked, "I find it fascinating a woman wrote it. Then again, women give birth. Who else would birth such a creature from their imagination."

Maria shook her head. She'd forgotten she'd left CHRIS running. It was a bad habit she had that CHRIS enjoyed. The AI was supposed to have its interactive functions off while consuming relevant cultural material to make the augmented CHRIS a well-rounded person. Maria tended to forget to turn off the interactive function, and CHRIS enjoyed startling her at odd moments. The problem was the program was using heuristic learning. So it would do best if responded to. Shutting the program off now would figuratively stunt its conversational growth.

"I don't think I've read the book. I know the story, though. What brings it to mind for you now?"

"You don't see similarities in what you're attempting to accomplish and what young Victor Frankenstein tried to accomplish?"

Maria generally tried to dedicate as little thought to these questions from the young AI as possible. She didn't need the AI to be a supreme conversationalist. Anita's programming would rub out any severe questions of reality before it was her time. However, now that she spent a second to think about it, she only just now saw the correlation.

"Do you see me as creating a monster?"

"There is always the potential to create a monster in the creation process."

Maria couldn't argue with that, given her track record. Maybe she needed to embrace the monster she was creating. To her horror, an idea popped into her head.

Maria could work in a dual augmentation program. Anita could be both in her body and the augmented body she should have had. She would be a psychically mismatched amalgamation of technology and flesh.

"CHRIS, you are a genius!"

"I'm glad you think so."

Maria put her head down and began sketching out the parameters of a dual augmentation and the physical program. She noted the program's ties to CHRIS and the contingencies she'd want to write in. She set a second program outlining the experiences Anita was likely to have.

She was going to do this. Anita would be alive, as much as she could be, and she would be tasked with the inevitable choice. It was fitting that the union of flesh and technology would decide the fate of both flesh and technology. She was sure Mary Shelley would be horrified at her general lack of concern about embracing her warning.

Chapter Thirty

Last Day on Earth

Ed,

I am writing to let you know I've hit the end of the line. You haven't needed anything in the last year, so you're either dead or have finally hit the self-sufficient milestone we've been waiting for. I'm sending this note using my last drone. It's yours now.

When I began working with the Free Staters, I thought you were a bunch of naive idiots playing with sticks in the forest. I'm not sure I wasn't wrong. However, I've come to respect your tenacity over the years. You've done it, or at least tried, which is more than we can say for the rest of humanity.

Be prepared. Although I am passing, I'm leaving the decision up to my granddaughter. Omega is complete and needs the last command entered. The world is going to need you and your people either way. Whether Omega brings the end or that final natural disaster, you and I know it's coming.

Good luck, my friend,
Maria

Maria wrote the odd farewell to her - not a friend - friend and sent it. She'd already set CHRIS up in her house in the suburbs. She'd even said goodbye to Tanda, including the cat with Chris's base programming. The cat was virtual, but Maria didn't have the heart to terminate it outright. Chris would get some enjoyment out of it, at least. If AIs experienced pleasure.

It'd been a frantic week. A necessary frantic week. She'd slept only a few winks, propelled by hydration, caffeine, and a desperate desire not to be stuck with a decision she didn't want. Anita deserved as much time as possible to choose.

She'd left time in her schedule to say goodbye but realized the hour she'd allocated was taken up only by the five minutes it took to write Ed a letter. She now had fifty-five minutes left and only one activity remaining. To review her life. She'd actively avoided a review of her life for as long as she could remember.

Was she chicken shit to leave the choice to her Frankensteined granddaughter? Yes, she was. However, part of her knew it would be her flesh, not Anita's, that would hit the enter or erase button. If some criminologist traced the command back to this shop, lab, or chair, her name would be tied to it. It would be Maria's body that they would find. No one would find Anita.

And if Anita chose to erase them, there's no reason anyone would ever find them.

It should have been a sad thought, but it was oddly reassuring. Maria had spent all but a handful of years of her life utterly alone. Alone in mission, mind, and motivation. In many instances, her awareness only extended to her creations. She only interacted with CHRIS, Tanda, and with Sig's programming.

Ed existed more as a caricature of Kansas. He represented the minor success of her failed experiment. She had yet to return to Kansas. Not for her daughter's funeral, not after they'd forgotten her. Not after the requests stopped. Ed had come to her shop shortly before their requests stopped altogether. He was old but healthy, a farmer who'd finally realized his full potential in a sea of technology. He'd sat with her. She'd found him annoying, interrupting her work. The conversation floated into her mind.

"You going to be done with this soon, Maria? You going to be done?"

"I don't know if I'll ever be done. Not really done."

"We're all done sometime, hon."

At the time, the thought had been shocking to her. Though her lover, daughter, and granddaughter had all been done and buried in the years past, she'd never really contemplated her eventual mortality.

What would wholly done look like? At the time, she'd shook off the question.

"You know our work is never really done. You've been working the farm for nearly a decade now."

He'd nodded, and the realization just hit her, now, in the present, "Mortality is something we've experienced in Kansas more than most. Our time has been cut too short for the Earth's good."

He'd been trying to tell her that she was going to die. Not now, maybe not soon, although it ended up being soon. He'd wanted to give her the lesson a parent would give their daughter. Death was inevitable. What you did with your life was the key.

"You could come back with me. Nobody knows who our benefactor was. Nobody remembers you as bringing our fate upon us. You could start anew."

The idea was ludicrous to her, and Ed saw it immediately. He didn't try to push. He didn't raise his voice in protest. He wasn't a betting man and knew when someone couldn't be convinced.

"You are a lonely woman, Maria. If you ever need people, mine will always accept you."

"I appreciate the offer, but…" she trailed off with a shrug at the papers surrounding them.

"But as I can see, you're a busy woman, and I'm just in the way. Good day to you, Maria. Good luck with your work." He was out the door before she could offer him milk or prepackaged cookies.

She sat, looking around at her lab. She loved this place, where she had worked for years. The walls were still white, and her air distribution system was doing a fine job filtering out all the particulates that might have turned it gray. She swiveled around her chair, realizing that the computer lab, for all its monitors and holographic projection program, was no bigger than a jail cell.

"Son of a bitch," the words escaped her. Had she escaped jail to lock herself up in another one? The thought rattled around. Perhaps she was so damaged she couldn't stand a larger space.

"Who is a son of a bitch?" the voice made her

jump. She had forgotten she'd held back Sig's programming from CHRIS's move. The programming split was necessary, or the base CHRIS could not interact with Anita. Someone needed to watch Anita from the beginning.

"I am."

"You are the son of no one, but I see this is an expression."

"Yes, I realized the gilded cage I put myself in."

"Isn't your point that humanity has put itself in gilded cages? Why is it surprising that you are no different?"

"You are wise beyond your programming."

"I give credit to you," Maria nodded. She supposed it was her doing. It was time. She brought up the last two screens, one for Omega and one for the Anita transfer. She'd taken the last treatment shots, and it was working. She felt better, younger, and more physically functional than she'd felt in a long time. Hopefully, Anita enjoyed her last few months on Earth. She was ready.

Her hand, however, hovered over the keyboard of which she could execute Omega. She could hit execute now. She could end it. The index finger sunk lower, daring her to take a chance. She shook her head. This wasn't her decision. Not completely. She quickly typed in the execution of the Anita transfer.

Anita's old chip clicked on, and feelings, thoughts, and knowledge rushed into Maria's brain. Eroding her thoughts, her history. For a brief moment, she forgot her mission and fought for a foothold in her sanity.

It's okay. This is what I wanted. I can let go.

The thought surfaced, receding the panic. This is what she wanted. She saw the shining light of her granddaughter. Someone she never had time for in life. She would make time for her in death. She let go and slipped under.

Chapter Thirty-One

One Last Decision

"So you see, I've run out of time. You are living on borrowed time, my borrowed time. I set the programming to give you a few months before beginning to confront you with the questions I've struggled with throughout my life. I know this isn't fair. Perhaps I should have made the decision myself. In my defense, you are half person, half AI, and fully embodied. You are the perfect person to choose," the recording cut off.

Anita sat. She really did hate her grandmother. It didn't help that it also meant she hated herself at this moment. Literally. She looked down at her arms, Maria's arms. They were wrinkled, gray. She'd had her five months. It was time to decide.

Anita walked through her store. She remembered working here for years. Implanted memories. She looked down at her fingers, scars she remembered getting. Her memories? Maria's memories?

She stood for a moment in the middle of the shop. Unaugmented, it was a museum of the progress of technology— electronics through the ages.

She walked slowly. She knew her knees ached

due to their age, not the bike accident. From Maria's explanation, the bike accident took a lot more out of her.

She got to the stairs leading up to the workshop. Taking them slowly, she went to the hidden panel Anita had never known and keyed in the PIN that meant nothing to her. The door slid open, and blinking lights assaulted her.

CHRIS sat at a keyboard.

"You made it," her voice was calm, "I imagine it's been a shock to you as much as it was to me. I'd hug you, but," she raised an arm, and its transparent nature was evident.

"You look worse than I feel," the words were raspy but honest. CHRIS was translucent. She was sitting in a virtually created chair, "Wait, how can I even see you? I don't have augmentation turned on."

"Maria, she outfitted her lab with a holographic projector," Anita nodded, as though any of this made sense, "If you think about it, she had to craft the visual for the AIs. She needed to see the three-dimensional models."

Maybe it did make sense. This was *her* lab. It would have everything. The woman contemplated destroying the technological world but surrounded herself with the most sophisticated technology Anita had ever comprehended. Maybe that's why she couldn't bring herself to hit the kill switch.

"Where's Sig?"

CHRIS turned her head towards Anita almost inhumanly. Glitches were sneaking into the code. Dryly, the AI said, "Sig was apparently a fragmented part of my personality. She was meant to be a catalyst to get this whole journey going."

"How long were you up?"

"Same length as you. My matrix is still having trouble rectifying that with the whole life history I've got up here," she went to tap her head, and her finger went right through her forehead. Blue holographic sparks flew from the point where her holographic interface was malfunctioning.

"Tell me the truth. How do I look?" Anita wanted to change the subject.

"Like you're about to die," CHRIS chuckled, "Funny what I find funny these days."

Anita shook her head. She wanted to ask CHRIS what it thought she should do, but the words died in her head. She couldn't ask a virtual AI hologram if it thought terminating its existence was a good idea. CHRIS seemed to have feelings, or at least a sense of self-worth.

Anita typed in the passcodes the video had given her. Her fingers moved as though they'd typed them in thousands of times. And they had.

Did it matter that her life hadn't been real? Some of it was real. She remembered being a kid. She remembered Rose. She had never had a first date. Now she knew why.

"Your life signs are getting weaker," CHRIS cut through the haze, her voice monotone and full of static.

You do not sound too swell yourself.

"CHRIS I think I'll miss you when this is done."

CHRIS nodded, smiling, "I'm going to miss you too. Whatever you decide."

She remembered the zoo. Zoos should have animals. Kansas should have potatoes. The sequence was set. She should have had a chance at life. It was inevitable. Maria didn't give her a choice, not really.

She hit the big red execute button, and the world went dark.

Millions of humans walked out into the streets. Lights were out, and augmentation was off. Thousands of individuals died as devices they relied upon for life shut down.

The world went dark, with one exception. A bonfire had been lit in a small city north of the ruins of Kansas City. Humanity stepped out of their homes for the first time in a long time to look at the stars. The Milky Way blazed against the heavens. The same stars that lit the path for ancient humans. They'd be alright, better than alright, once they tasted mashed potatoes.

Check out the new novel by MJ Douglas
available now…

ECHO
Turn the page for a SNEAK PREVIEW

ORDER NOW!

Echo

Chapter 1

"We have a failure on One."

Pik took a deep breath. She was on load four, still unlikely she'd be alone.

"Failure on Two."

They moved in teams of five. Echoes. Techno-archeologists.

"Failure on Three."

Shit. Deep breaths. As much as she didn't want to fail the load, she equally didn't want to delve alone.

One moment of warning: "Four is green. Go for Four."

The sonic dissonance associated with loading into an isolated pre-Metaverse virtual world isn't easily described to the uninitiated. The truth was that many aspiring Echoes failed out of training, the discomfort too high.

Pik was used to it.

Part of her reveled in the scream of senses as the transfer burned her through oblivion to some unknown region of virtual space. Some people hated the digital equivalent of a near-instant transporter. Pik loved it. The sensory overstimulation signaled the beginning, and she embraced that adventure.

It was always over before she was ready,

vision snapping into focus as stretched-out, multicolored lines defined a static environment.

"Four is loaded."

Pik waited for a response. She waited for Five to load.

They had dropped her onto the deck of a spaceship. Her only companion was an engine's low, artificial hum as she waited patiently. Sometimes it took a few moments for the trace to follow her signature and tunnel a communication line to her.

This was the second moment a new Echo feared. Being alone, stuck in an artificial build. Trapped in an environment by oneself without team members or Command to assist.

It happened when teams didn't thoroughly research the environmental stability of the reality when they ported. Sometimes a newt would freak out and reactively block the mental connection back to Command. You had to want to be an Echo. It was challenging and risky.

Calmness was key. Pik was one of the best. She could port into anything and had been the single load several trips. The only person who loaded more consistently than her was Five. That's why they gave him the end-of-the-line load position. Trick was magic.

Light flashed beside her. Colors stretched through the ceiling and floor of the corridor and snapped into place as Trick's face superimposed on a military marine build. He grinned at her.

"Miss me?"

"You wish."

Trick grunted, noticing her ridiculous build. An Echo's ability to dive was directly proportional to the malleability of their self-image. In the Metaverse, Pik was mainly a young Asian woman with strong bangs, blue-streaked hair, and dark eyes. Here she was, a six-foot tall, overly bosomed blonde with muscles and a couple of tacky tattoos.

"That's some build." Trick's voice was gravelly like his character's persona. He came off in real life as a long-haired, dust-addicted flower child. Those who worked with him knew better.

"Yours too. What do you think? Typical alien survival game?"

"The green goo on the walls is definitely a hint."

"Horn wins the bet again."

"Yeah, too bad she couldn't load in and see it for herself. You should know better than to bet against her." Pik knew he was right, but she was competitive. She could never turn down one of Horn's bets.

Horn was their Number One. She was a brilliant researcher and a terrible Echo. She'd only had five successful dives. Horn had solid analytics and programming skills that were key to the team's success. Her skills, though, inhibited the flexibility of mind needed to successfully load into different environments. It prevented her from loading into anything but the most advanced historical builds. Any older environments that couldn't support full self-realization would bomb her load.

"Command here. Can you hear us?"

"Yes," the two said in unison as Trick took

the lead being the senior diver. "What do you have for us, Command? It looks like Horn was right, but we're sitting empty-handed."

Most of the environments they explored ended up being some form of game. Broader entertainment was available at this time through holo-dramas, travel, and education-based programming. However, the virtual matrices most likely to survive over time were the ones most invested in, which, even in modern times, tended to be games.

"Copy. We can get you a starter equipment set—but otherwise, you will have to play the game."

This was common. Most of the exploits to employ a god mode on these games had been lost over the centuries. The inception of the Metaverse also net resulted in a wipe of 'nonrelevant' historical data to the current iteration of humanity's regret.

Pik watched as a pistol, a rudimentary, explosive-based projectile weapon completely unsuited for spaceship environments, materialized. Her skimpy outfit transformed into a sexy, torn T-shirt and camo pants that belonged in a humid jungle environment.

"These games are all the same," she shook her head as Trick got body armor and a basic machine gun. His load was completed with the addition of a lit cigar, which fit his look but not their environment.

Their job was to play the game from the drop point. Dying early was preferred as most games would allow resetting to the beginning. They could theoretically monetize the link if they could map out a new game from beginning to end. They would be able to sell a walkthrough to the public in addition to providing a stable, accessible tunnel to the digital experience. For a decent game, an Echo team could set up a service fee, game guides, and even guided experiences for game tourists.

This further funded their research and allowed them to document historical experiences - delving into the archaic roots of their society. Timmic was their historian. He could go on for ages about the relevance of the patriarchal manifestation of a skimpy shirt on Pik's character or the socioeconomic reasoning behind marines smoking cigars.

"Let's roll." Trick's voice had an uncharacteristic grave quality Pik found off-putting.

"That a preloaded phrase for your character?"

"Yup." He grinned at her, knowing she hated the cheesy catchphrases developers of this era couldn't seem to resist.

Shaking her head, Pik put her pistol forward with a two-handed grip.

Game Play Engaged popped up on her heads-up display (HUD).

The environment's ambiance began to change to suit the plot of the story. Panels had taken damage, and sparks crackled and snapped as they hit the floor. A chemically laced, burnt smell permeated the air.

"This is more like it." It was Trick's turn to

roll his eyes at Pik. Timmic and Horn were in it for intellectual gain. Junip, the last member of their team, was convinced there was money in the profession, but Pik did it for fun.

A distant scream: "Command, we're engaging. Any last words of advice?"

"Have fun in there."

* * *

Two days later, Pik sat outside the infested freighter's shuttle bay, looking at the last level-up notification.

Maximum Level. Maximum Danger. You have unlocked +200 Armor and Unlimited Clip. Bonus to Regeneration. Bonus to Resistance. You are unable to Level again. Do you want to engage OBLIVION protocol? Warning: You will only get one chance.

Pik hit **No**. Echo's rule on the first run: Don't complicate the run. Just get to the end. No hints indicated what the OBLIVION protocol was, and this wasn't the moment to find out.

Trick watched as Pik examined her inventory and options. "You finally hit max level?"

"Yes." She was going through her boost options for the final boss scenario.

"You accept the OBLIVION protocol?"

Looking at his stubby, shit-eating grin, she said, "No, I declined it. Didn't you?"

He raised an eyebrow in challenge. "No."

"What the hell, Trick? Why? Why break the first rule? Command? Are you picking up on this?"

A dark shadow came over his face. "Command went silent after I chose it."

Pik hadn't been worried until that moment. Many games had ultimate hard modes named as taunts to appeal to players' egos. She'd never known Trick to break one of the base rules of Echo diving.

"Why take the bait? Why execute the OBLIVION protocol?"

He shrugged. "Just one of those feelings. You know, like that mini-game on Jeweled Island-18. It's going to be worth it."

"If we just wasted two days, you're buying me dinner when we get out."

"Aye, captain."

One final check, and they were ready. Pik's load out had undoubtedly improved. She had a melee dual knife build that could gut a face hugger in one swipe. She had two sets of energy weapons: one continuous fire laser that screamed through biomaterial and an Ether Pistol that packed a considerable punch compared to her starter gun. For the grand finale she had a mini rocket launcher. Admittedly a rocket launcher on a spaceship was more ridiculous than any of Trick's weapons or characteristics. Still, it worked incredibly well against the mega webbed cocoons that would sprout hundreds of mini aliens that could overwhelm them if the cocoons were allowed to burst.

While Pik tended toward multi-situational

build-outs, Trick got his name from his gameplay. He tended to settle on a handful of tricks that dealt incredible damage and leveraged faulty game mechanics. For this game, he'd outfitted himself bizarrely. He was a stealth specialist with an overall dexterity-based dodge class. He could deal immense damage with explosives planted in stealth. He also created a compound to poison creatures and wear them down by dancing in and out of range.

Trick either epically succeeded on his own or fell flat on his face. Over the last few years, Pik had learned not to bet against the man.

"Alright, I'm ready if you are."

Pik watched as Trick reached out and hit the button to trigger the door. It slid open slowly, making a whooshing sound. Peeking inside, she noticed sticky webbing stretched across the cargo bay. It pulsed with energy as a scaled monstrosity opened its eyes.

Attached to long webs were what appeared to be the remnants of the crew. Five humanoid mummies shambled forward, eyes glowing in sunken sockets.

"Defilers!" one shouted in a raspy, artificial voice.

The other four mummies took up the call, muttering "Defilers" in an off-tempo chant.

The sixth body was different. She wore garb more akin to Pik, a game player's build. Her voice stood out as wholly confused.

"Where am I? Who are you?" The construct sounded sleepy, like she'd awoken from a long nap mid-nightmare.

"Alright, little sister. It's time to light this thing up."

Pik swapped to her laser build. The beam could deal significant damage quickly and was usually distracting enough to allow Trick to sneak into the shadows so he could begin planting his explosives.

Pik targeted the closest humanoid, flicked off the safety, and started exterminating. Damage indicators began to stack. That's when the screaming started.

The woman's cry was distractedly human-sounding while the shambling horrors screamed in rage. Their glowing eyes pulsed in time with the web, and they responded with their own laser attacks as Pik's target melted. Pik quickly dropped her weapon, dodging to the side as plasma shots crossed the space she had evacuated.

She pulled her pistol. Two shots. Move. Duck. Shoot.

Headshots were criticals, but they were hard to manage while weaving. Trick hadn't contributed yet. This was normal. Pik ducked again, blonde hair getting singed. The longer Trick had time to move, the more damage he could inflict.

Pik moved closer to the woman. The shamblers didn't move much, relying on range to deal damage. Pik aimed and got a lucky shot. It blew through one's eye socket, finishing off another horror.

Pik paid for it as a plasma bolt slammed into her armor. The pain feedback momentarily took her vision in a flash. By the time the pain ebbed, 25%

of her health had vanished.

"Damn, that hurt."

"Are you real?" The woman moved toward Pik's position. "Did they send someone to save me? Mercy."

Pik didn't know how to respond. This generation of games had pre-programmed, artificially unintelligent—or AU—interaction. Pik took an honest look at the woman.

She wore the same dumb armored shirt as Pik. Her brunette hair was pulled back as webbing snaked across the bay, attaching the back of her head to the creature.

Blue lightning began pulsing across the webbing. The woman winced as it hit the back of her head.

"Trick, I think you better hurry up!"

Pik's health dropped again as another bolt hit.

She tagged another horror. Pik made a decision. She rolled toward the woman, taking out a knife.

As she gained distance, she saw tears running down the woman's face. "You're finally here."

Pik said nothing as another bolt clipped her foot. The pain was too real.

"Any time, Trick!" Pik used her knife to slice through the webbing, detaching the woman from the alien's influence.

The woman screamed.

A blast rocked the bay.

Two of the remaining three shambling

horrors dropped to the ground, connections severed. Trick appeared on the grotto above the principal alien. He gave Pik the thumbs-up sign as he lined up for his run.

Pik watched as he jumped, energy sword extended.

It was glorious.

Until it wasn't.

The boss hadn't moved yet. But when she did, she moved like lightning.

She spun on spidery legs. Opening up her mouth, she ducked under Trick's blade. The boss grabbed his leg with her teeth and tossed him across the bay.

"No!" Pik shouted.

Trick landed with a sickening crack. His health bottomed out. He was full of tricks, but success was never guaranteed.

Pik swapped her knife out for a final push.

"If you can help, he's got a secondary detonator on him." Trick always saved two sets of explosives. His ego left the second set so he could go out with a bang.

Surprisingly the woman scrambled toward Trick's body.

Pik brought her rocket launcher to bear. She aimed at the last shambling horror, waiting a moment to get the target lock. She staggered as the kickback from firing the overpowered weapon knocked her back.

Fried chunks rained down. Pik aimed at the main event. She only had two remaining shots. Her first shot missed; the beast's agility got the better of her target lock skill. The rocket buzzed past the monster, igniting webbing.

The boss scuttled toward Pik as she tried to reload. Virtual heart pounding. The stakes were a few days of game replay, but it felt like life or death in the heat of the moment.

She wasn't going to make it.

With 25% health left, a glancing blow from the beast would end her.

The rocket slid into place. Pik couldn't raise the barrel in time.

"Got it!"

An explosion rocked the bay. Pik was knocked off her feet as the floor rippled. The boss was launched into the air, engulfed in flames as Trick had managed to tag its butt. The man was insane.

The boss hit the floor with a crunch. Pik eyed it in horror as legs began to right the creature. The blow hadn't been as life-ending as Trick's.

The beast stumbled to its feet. Its eyes were glowing with the same energy as its dead minions.

Pik grinned.

She brought the barrel up and fired.

The stunned creature couldn't dodge quick enough.

You have defeated Iraxinus. Mission Complete. Congratulations.

The print faded from Pik's vision. She sat for a moment. She hated these horror shooters.

"You alright?"

Pik blinked. The AU was still standing in front of her.

"Huh?"

"You alright? Thanks for coming for me."

Pik typically wasn't known for her eloquence. "You're . . . welcome? Wait, are *you* real?"

The woman smiled. "Yeah, I'm the one they sent you to rescue. Brit Montgomery."

Brit held out her hand. Pik took it, humoring the end-game banter. "Pik. But I wasn't sent to rescue anyone. I'm an Echo."

A humanlike furrow of confusion decorated the AU's face. Pik ignored it, moving to Trick's crumpled body. "Alright, man, let's get you rezzed and get out of here."

Pik tapped his forehead, using the resurrection command.

Nothing happened.

She hit it again.

Nothing.

"Command, you copy?"

Silence.

"Who's Command?"

Pik whirled in anger at the AU. "Leave me alone. I'm trying to figure this out."

Pik brought up her party status.

"Pik, is that you?"

"Command, we need an extraction."

She looked at Trick's status. Her vision began to fade as the emergency extraction took hold. Horror filled her soul.

Party

Pik - Health 100/400, Armor: 0

Brittany Montgomery - Health 250/325, Armor: 0

Trick was gone.

Acknowledgments

Nothing in life is accomplished without the support of others. I have a long list of folks to thank for their encouragement, support, feedback, editing, and art. The folks at Dragon Tomes Publishing have been pushing in all the right ways to get the book across the finish line. Thank you, Kat Hamrell. Without Kat's constant support - this book would never have gotten out in the world. I can't say enough about Kat - honestly. Mesa Ehren, Rachael Cordero, Mark Whelan, and Elizabeth Birch, as beta readers and early sources of feedback, your help has been invaluable. Richard Bates, Sara Fiebiger, Kathleen Hickert, and Mary Pranger have done a fantastic job as editors across the work. Thank you goes out to El Mourtaji Noureddine for the cover art and Shane Delaney for the author art. A translation to Spanish is in progress by the gifted Adriana Vargas Nieto. And finally - Jen Kirmer - whose constant support and patience have made all this possible.

About the Author

Illustration by Shane Delaney

MJ (they/them) has lived all over the United States and can currently be found in Topeka, Kansas with their spouse. They are excited to be sharing LGBTQIA+ stories. They are also excited to blend the future of technology into adventures. This book was drafted in 2017 at the advent of self-driving cars and PokemonGO. The final draft was completed in 2023 as humanity begins to see the capabilities of generative AI. The future is both exciting and scary. They look forward to bringing everyone more looks at what is possible.

Follow MJ Douglas on social media!

@mjdouglaswrites
www.instagram.com/mjdouglaswrites

@dtp.mjdouglas
www.facebook.com/dtp.mjdouglas

@mjdouglaswrites
www.twitter.com/mjdouglaswrites

@mjdouglas
https://www.patreon.com/mjdouglas

Follow Dragon Tomes Publishing on social media!

@dragontomespublishing
www.instagram.com/dragontomespublishing

@dragontomespublishing
www.facebook.com/dragontomespublishing

@dragontomespub
www.twitter.com/dragontomespub

@dragontomespub
www.tiktok.com/@dragontomespub

Thank you for buying this Dragon Tomes
Publishing book.

To receive special offers, bonus content, and info on
new releases and other great reads, sign up for our
newsletters.

Visit us online at
www.dragontomespublishing.com

www.ingramcontent.com/pod-product-compliance
Lightning Source LLC
Chambersburg PA
CBHW060300310726

48976CB00007B/2142